RIDE TO TERROR...

As my horse trotted down the road between tall forest growths, a shot rang out. My horse suddenly collapsed, dropping to her front knees and propelling me over her head to land with stunning force.

I couldn't get up. I knew I must, because danger was closing in all around me. But every muscle was paralyzed. Then I saw the horse, lying on her side, legs twitching in what seemed to be a dying agony, and I struggled to my feet.

I was stumbling toward the protection of the forest when the second bullet sang its deadly song a few yards from me. I plunged into the forest and, heart pounding with fear, staggered on until I could go no further. I collapsed, unable to move another step. And as I lay there helpless, I heard footsteps approaching...

SIGNET Gothics You'll Enjoy

- [ ] **VALLEY OF SHADOWS** by Dorothy Daniels. (#E9030—$1.75)*
- [ ] **THE CORMAC LEGEND** by Dorothy Daniels. (#J8655—$1.95)*
- [ ] **THE LANDSEND TERROR** by Julia Trevelyan. (#E8526—$1.75)*
- [ ] **GREYTHORNE** by Julia Trevelyan. (#W7802—$1.50)
- [ ] **THE TOWER ROOM** by Julia Trevelyan. (#E8711—$1.75)*
- [ ] **LEGACY OF FEAR** by Virginia Coffman. (#E8860—$1.75)*
- [ ] **THE CLIFFS OF DREAD** by Virginia Coffman. (#E8301—$1.75)*
- [ ] **THE EVIL AT QUEEN'S PRIORY** by Virginia Coffman. (#E8403—$1.75)*
- [ ] **SIGNET DOUBLE GOTHIC—CURSE OF THE ISLAND POOL** by Virginia Coffman and **THE HIGH TERRACE** by Virginia Coffman. (#J9126—$1.95)*
- [ ] **ISLE OF THE UNDEAD** by Virginia Coffman. (#W8032—$1.50)
- [ ] **MIST AT DARKNESS** by Virginia Coffman. (#Q6138—95¢)
- [ ] **NIGHT AT SEA ABBEY** by Virginia Coffman. (#W8093—$1.50)
- [ ] **THE BROKEN KEY** by Mary Linn Roby. (#Y6766—$1.25)
- [ ] **THE CURSE OF THE CONCULLENS** by Florence Stevenson. (#W7228—$1.50)
- [ ] **A SHADOW ON THE HOUSE** by Florence Stevenson. (#Y6520—$1.25)

* Price slightly higher in Canada

Buy them at your local bookstore or use this convenient coupon for ordering.

THE NEW AMERICAN LIBRARY, INC.,
P.O. Box 999, Bergenfield, New Jersey 07621

Please send me the SIGNET BOOKS I have checked above. I am enclosing $_____ (please add 50¢ to this order to cover postage and handling). Send check or money order—no cash or C.O.D.'s. Prices and numbers are subject to change without notice.

Name _____

Address _____

City_____ State_____ Zip Code_____

Allow 4-6 weeks for delivery.
This offer is subject to withdrawal without notice.

Bridal Black

Dorothy Daniels

A SIGNET BOOK
NEW AMERICAN LIBRARY
TIMES MIRROR

NAL BOOKS ARE AVAILABLE AT QUANTITY DISCOUNTS WHEN USED TO PROMOTE PRODUCTS OR SERVICES. FOR INFORMATION PLEASE WRITE TO PREMIUM MARKETING DIVISION, THE NEW AMERICAN LIBRARY, INC., 1633 BROADWAY, NEW YORK, NEW YORK 10019.

Copyright © 1980 by Dorothy Daniels

All rights reserved

SIGNET TRADEMARK REG. U.S. PAT. OFF. AND FOREIGN COUNTRIES
REGISTERED TRADEMARK—MARCA REGISTRADA
HECHO EN CHICAGO, U.S.A.

SIGNET, SIGNET CLASSICS, MENTOR, PLUME, MERIDIAN AND NAL BOOKS *are published by The New American Library, Inc., 1633 Broadway, New York, New York 10019*

FIRST PRINTING, MAY, 1980

1 2 3 4 5 6 7 8 9

PRINTED IN THE UNITED STATES OF AMERICA

1

It was one of those unusual late-winter noontimes when the sun is warm, as if the weather anticipated the coming spring and I was taking advantage of it by settling myself on one of the benches in Central Park near Seventy-second Street and West Drive. This was a considerable distance from my place of employment, but I enjoyed the walk and I was granted more than an hour of leisure time. This was exceptional in that most office employees were granted from twenty minutes to half an hour for their midday respite.

I didn't carry my noonday meal, as most girls did. Where I worked, I was able to order a fine meal if I chose, and eat it under very comfortable conditions.

I carried no newspaper or book. All I wanted to do was sit here in the sunlight and enjoy myself. Hansom cabs, ornate carriages, and landaus passed by, for West Drive was a busy place. A few lumbering wagons passed also, though I understood there was some sort of law against these noisy vehicles using Central Park as a thoroughfare. But then, I thought they did little harm and we were living in a modern world these days. It was now four years since we'd come into the twentieth century. I remembered that New Year's Day, for the celebrations had been extensive as this was no ordinary New Year's Day but the beginning of a new century that promised to be exciting and interesting. Papa and Mama had taken me to Chelsea Place, where a lavish parade passed by. I was fourteen then and old enough to both enjoy the spectacle and appreciate its meaning.

Now, four years later, Papa and Mama were both dead. I lived alone in a small room at my place of work. I missed Papa and Mama, but otherwise I thought I was indeed a fortunate girl.

As I sat there idly watching passersby, a few men and one woman rode past on horseback, keeping to the paved drive. Another horseman who was coming up very fast was using the green area and his mount was kicking up plenty of sod. Yet he sat his horse well, handled the animal like someone born to it, and the horse appeared to be enjoying the run.

He was almost opposite me when his riding derby flew off. He clapped a hand to his head as if to rescue it, but of course, the hat was already sailing through the air. I laughed at the expression on the rider's face. It was one of exasperation and frustration. I got up, ran over to where the hat finally settled, and I held it up for him to see as he looked back.

He raised a hand that he understood. He came back, slowly this time. As he neared me, I tried to hand him the hat, but he shook his head.

"Set it down on the grass, please, and then stand back," he called out.

I was puzzled as to this request, but I obeyed it, placed the derby on the ground, and got out of the way. He rode a considerable distance, turned the horse, and urged the animal to its fastest speed. As he neared the hat, he leaned far out of the saddle and scooped it up with a flourish. I couldn't resist clapping my hands in admiration of the feat. He was certainly a horseman who knew how to ride. He turned the horse and returned to the bench where I was again seated. He dismounted, let the horse graze on the park grass, and he came over to bow before me.

"I do thank you, miss. The derby is one I always wear when I ride. I swear it is lucky for me because I've never had an accident since I've owned the hat. And now look what it did for me. I've met a pretty girl. May I sit down?"

"Why, certainly," I said. "This is a public park. Besides, I enjoyed your bit of showmanship. You are a splendid rider."

"Well, I should be. Do you ride?"

"No, I never have. I was born and grew up in the city."

"You've missed something. It's great sport. Look here, if you're not one of those lofty types, may I introduce myself?"

"You may, sir," I said. I was already intrigued by him. I judged his age to be about twenty-seven or -eight. He was quite tall, not much short of six feet, and solidly built. His eyes were an amber color, I thought, though I hadn't dared look into them for fear of being called coquettish. He had a bold, quite handsome face with a firm chin and a no-nonsense mouth. His hair was as black as a raven.

"I'm Alex Paige. I live in Virginia. I breed and train horses there."

"Well, no wonder you ride so well. I am Amy Wilton."

"You're also a rather amazing girl," he said.

"In what way, may I ask?"

"I've been in the city for a month, business and pleasure. A man can get very lonely in a big city like this, but good heavens, when I look sideways at a girl, she will nod the first time I see her. Perhaps smile a little the second time, and on the third occasion, will deliberately turn her head away. It's frustrating to say the least."

I smiled. "If you'd spoken the third time, those heads would not have turned away. I assure you the girl you were trying to meet was perhaps as anxious as you, but so terribly bound by convention. That's how we were raised, sir. To be outrageously bashful—on the surface."

He threw his head back and laughed. "Thank heaven I'm at last getting an education. I suppose the same thing happens in Virginia. I've been kept so busy these last two or three years that I haven't had time to notice."

"You really raise and train horses?" I asked. "For racing, perhaps? My father loved horse racing."

"He was then, madam, a gentleman, for the love of horse racing is the ultimate criterion by which a gentleman can be judged. How does he do with his wagering?"

"He never went to the track to bet, only to study the horses and get terribly excited during the races. He always said it didn't take betting to do that."

"He was right. By heavens, he was perfectly right. You speak of him . . ."

I nodded. "He died four years ago. So did my mother."

"We've a great deal in common, Miss Wilton. I lost my father and two brothers. I did gain a stepfather, whom I detest, and some assorted relatives I cannot say I care for. So it seems we are alone in the world, as far as family affection is concerned. Perhaps we should console ourselves at supper. I do owe you something for rescuing my hat."

"I'm afraid not, Mr. Paige. I'm afraid I'm not quite that modern."

"Oh, come now, I mean no harm. You can't accuse me of flirting with you. This is a matter of business.

I owe you for rescuing my hat, and I did note that you were not the type to turn your head away even at the first meeting if not the third."

"I have always been taught that one should be properly introduced," I said.

"Well, I can't do much about that. I don't know many people in this city. The only place that knows me is a hotel. I stay at the Plaza."

I covered my lips to restrain the laugh. "Then, sir, I think we may be safely introduced."

He looked puzzled. "I'm afraid I don't understand. . . ."

"I work at the Plaza. I am a bookkeeper and typist there. I even live there, so we do have a friend in common. I will have supper with you, Mr. Paige, for the Hotel Plaza can be my chaperon."

"We shall be most discreet." He chuckled. "The Plaza can ruin a reputation very quickly. May I walk you back?"

"You'd look positively silly walking with me down Fifth Avenue, with your horse following us."

"I've got to teach horses to go home by themselves," he said. "May I call for you at—say—eight?"

"You may meet me in the lobby at eight," I said. "Visitors are not allowed above the eighteenth floor and I live on the nineteenth."

"At eight then," he said. "I'm looking forward to it. I assure you it will be the first truly enjoyable meal I shall have since arriving in New York."

I gave him my hand and let him hold it a moment. He was looking deeply into my eyes and I could almost feel the warmth behind his, now clearly an amber color.

I had felt many a girlhood thrill at meeting a nice boy, but it had never struck me quite like this. I should have removed my hand from his rather tight grasp, but I couldn't do so. I forgot all the niceties of social etiquette, and at that moment I wouldn't have given a darn if I did remember.

"At eight," I said. "I must get back."

"Yes . . . of course," he said. "I'm sorry. It's just that . . . well, we seem to have hit it off rather well and . . . to be very frank . . . I like you. Everything about you. I shall look forward to eight this evening."

He clamped on his derby, called to the horse, and went over to the animal. He mounted, as I began my walk back to the hotel. I looked over my shoulder. He yanked off the derby, brought it up and then down, accompanied by a wild yell. I shook my head and laughed a little, and I didn't feel quite as alone in the world as I had twenty minutes ago.

The Plaza, of course, maintained a dress shop for the convenience of guests. It was expensive and carried only the loveliest of frocks. Marion Stuart, the woman who ran it, was a good friend of mine. I often did typewriter work for her as a gesture of friendship, always refusing to take money for it. I went back to the office where I worked, but in the middle of the afternoon I'd finished one segment of the week's bookkeeping and I took a few minutes off to visit the dress shop. Marion Stuart was a gracious, amenable woman of about thirty. Slim and a lovely brunette.

"Marion," I said, "I have a favor to ask. A most important favor and perhaps an impertinent one."

"You've met a young man," she said promptly, perhaps from her experiences over her years.

"How did you ever guess? He's invited me to supper. Right here in the hotel. He lives here for the time being. He's from Virginia."

"And you wish to borrow a gown. Now it just happens that I've several in your size. I ordered them to show to a countess from Belgium, but she's away and won't return for a week. So we can safely utilize one of these; they are superb—and your size. You'll be fascinating in any one of them. So we'll get busy right now. Try them on and take your pick. If it doesn't fit, we'll make it fit."

I spent twenty hurried minutes, but it wasn't necessary to try on all of them. I fell in love with the third one I tried on. It was a gown of peach satin, trimmed with lace and velvet ribbon. The waistline was small, but fortunately, so were my measurements. It was the kind of gown I might have dreamed about, but I never thought I'd wear one so beautiful—even if it was borrowed.

Hugo, who ran the elevator that rose to the nineteenth floor, was known for his total disregard concerning gowns, jewelry, and perfumes, so when his eyes opened wide as I stepped into the car, I took that as a sign of approval. I was ecstatic about the way I looked. I never was vain, but I knew this gown suited me.

However, as I stepped out of the car on the main floor, I held my breath. It was exactly eight o'clock and there he stood, facing the elevator. He looked as if he'd been standing there a long time. He was definitely handsome in white tie and tails. His eyes grew wider too. He took my gloved hand and bowed over it.

"You are beautiful," he said. "Some man might say you have made his evening by your presence. I will say you have made my life—and take that any way you please. I assure you it is only a compliment."

"Thank you," I said. "I will happily consider it as such. And may I say you certainly are handsome in evening dress, sir. Although I will admit you also look good in a derby."

He grinned, took my arm, and marched me into the larger of the two dining rooms. The maître d' looked a bit surprised when he recognized me, but he merely smiled and made no issue of it. He led us to a reserved table, one from which I could view almost the entire room.

"Where I come from," he said, "we drink bourbon and water."

"Sherry for me," I said.

"But champagne with supper?"

"I would enjoy it, Mr. Paige."

"I took the liberty of ordering supper so we would be served only the very best. Chateaubriand, and you may tell the waiter how you wish it done. As far as I am concerned whatever way you like it is the way I like it."

I gave the necessary information to the captain and we were alone for a few minutes until the waiter returned with the drinks.

"What will we talk about?" he asked.

He was so comfortable to be with. "Have you met our chaperon?" I asked. "She is nineteen stories high, she cost twelve million five hundred thousand dollars at birth. She has marble stairways—five of them. There are two dining rooms and they employ one hundred cooks."

"Well, you are familiar with her, I must say."

"I keep the books on the one hundred chefs and many of the other employees too. Now that's over with, please tell me something about your . . . is it a ranch?"

"We call it a farm. I may as well tell you, I'm quite wealthy. That was not of my doing, but my father's and his father's before him. The farm is large. We don't raise crops, only horses."

"It must be wonderful, out of the city," I said with a sigh. "The city is all I've ever known. Oh, there were vacations, and I enjoyed them, but I've never had the pleasure of a lengthy stay."

The drinks arrived. The waiter withdrew and we raised glasses and looked at each other across the table.

Alex said, "Before this goes any further—before we toast something or other—may I see you again? Often?"

Somewhat sadly I told him I couldn't afford it. "The gown was loaned to me by the owner of the dress shop in the hotel. I couldn't wear the same gown . . . you will understand that, please."

"Oh, yes, I understand it. I think it's all a lot of nonsense. A lovely gown, such as you wear now, doesn't grow any less lovely the second time. Or the third or fourth. However, I know what you mean. Still, if you were able to afford it, would you have supper with me again?"

"I should be delighted," I said.

"We could go to some other place where the gown hasn't been seen. . . ."

"Actually it was ordered by someone else," I explained. "I don't own it."

"Oh. Well, then, perhaps to a place not as fashionable as this?"

"I should be very happy, Mr. Paige."

"Oh, damn," he said, "call me Alex, will you?"

"Of course, Alex. When will you be going home?"

"I halfway planned that I'd leave tomorrow, but then . . . something happened."

"Oh?" I said, bracing myself.

"Yes—my derby blew off."

I raised my glass. "Here's to the derby," I said, and we both laughed and soon we were talking avidly about my life in the city and his in the country.

We didn't leave the restaurant until after eleven. This was the more formal room; the other restaurant was also used for dancing. When we walked into the lobby and heard the music, we went there and danced until far after midnight. We didn't talk very much as we danced. I think we were all talked out, but the lack of conversation didn't detract from the pleasure of the evening.

He saw me to the elevator, looked at me with a longing expression. It was strange, two people meeting accidentally, and after our first evening together, both loath to leave the other. I'd rarely been as happy. In my room I carefully hung up the gown, got ready for bed, and lay awake a long time thinking about Alex. I came to the conclusion that he was the nicest man I'd ever met. So considerate, kind, attentive. And yet there was also a rugged quality about him that I admired. He was seemingly out of his element in the city, but he accepted the new kind of life as graciously as if he'd been born here.

In the morning it all seemed like a lovely dream, but it was real enough. At midmorning Marion, from the dress shop, came into the office and whispered in my ear.

"All those gowns . . . they were paid for by a young man who ordered them delivered to your room. I didn't know what to do. They were ordered for someone else, but he wanted to pay double . . . triple . . . anything. . . ."

"Oh, Marion, I can't accept them. And you can't afford to sell them. You'll get in trouble. . . ."

"No, I wouldn't. That's why I came to see you. I can get others. The customer has no idea what I've selected for her and she has so much money and so many gowns she won't care anyway. I could use the business, dear."

"I don't know, Marion. I met this man only yesterday—by accident no less. He's wonderful. I've never met anyone so considerate and so much fun to be with. Why, last night we had supper and stayed very late. Then we went dancing. I felt as if I'd been introduced to a new kind of life...."

Marion stepped back and looked at me critically. "I'd say you fell in love with him."

"Oh, Marion, after one night?"

"He's certainly in love with you. That I'm sure of."

"Of course he isn't. It doesn't happen that way."

"It doesn't happen that way—often," she corrected me. "What'll I do about the gowns?"

"I'm seeing him again tonight and I'll come to an understanding. Those gowns are worth more than I make in a year. How can I accept them? I'll let you know."

"Well, they're in your room," she said. "He paid me in cash. I'll put the money aside in case you decide not to accept them, but I'd wear the blue one tonight. You'll knock him dead, although I think he's mortally wounded already. Good luck, dear. See me tomorrow morning."

I finished my work. I'm not sure how I did, but I finally closed the last ledger, removed the paper cuffs from my arms, put my desk in order, and went to my room.

There I sat at the window that overlooked the park and I thought it the most wonderful public park in the world. But I didn't know if I was prepared for this whirlwind courtship that I knew was beginning. I liked Alex. I closed my eyes and thought about him. Not about his money, or even his good looks. I thought only of him as a man. And when I opened my eyes I knew I was in love with him.

At supper I wore the blue and he was elated. "I was worried you'd not accept them," he said. "It was a rather bold gesture on my part, but . . . I do wish to see you as often as I can."

"I don't know if I will keep them, Alex. It isn't being done. . . ."

"Hang etiquette," he said. "Keep them. Even if you never see me again, which won't happen unless you can run very fast, very far, for I'll be right behind you. May I say something all out of turn, far too personal?"

"Of course, Alex."

"I'm in love with you. I fell in love as I rode past the bench where you were sitting. Sometimes I think my derby knew it and blew off on purpose. Are you offended?"

"Alex, of course I'm not. You have just paid me the greatest compliment of my life."

"Uh-huh," he said. "May I ask how you feel about me?"

"I love you very much," I said.

"Will you marry me?"

"Yes, I'll marry you, Alex darling. And all my life I'll bless that derby hat. Oh, Alex, how did this happen? Is it real? Are we just making this up?"

"After supper I'd like to take a ride in the park," he said. "I want to talk to you. It's very important to me."

I thought he ate rather hastily because the importance of the talk he suggested seemed that great. He hailed a carriage. It was pleasant, and even in this gown I'd be comfortable enough. When the carriage entered the park, passing through the area where the lights were either dim or absent, I never knew which, he took me in his arms and kissed me for the first time, and if there was an iota of doubt in my mind, it fled from me then. I knew that I loved him with all my heart.

"I asked you to marry me," he said. "I take it back and I will ask you again, after we talk. I don't want you marrying me under any false ideas."

"What on earth are you trying to say?" I asked in fresh dismay.

"It's not me I'll talk about. You know all there is to know about me. If you will excuse the indelicacy, it's my damned family I must talk about."

"Alex," I said, "is it as bad as that?"

"Listen and judge for yourself. My mother, as a widow, fell for the enchantment projected by the man who became my stepfather. Gordon Holbert promised her a life of pleasure, and gave her cruelty, neglect, and insincerity. Mother began drinking and she is now somewhat of a problem. I think Gordon hopes she will soon die so he can inherit the farm—he thinks."

"Alex, can that be true? Can such a man exist?"

"There are hordes of them, darling. But he's fooling himself. Mother soon sensed what she married and the farm is in my name alone."

"Is your stepfather that cruel and unfaithful?"

"He is. Then there is my uncle, Len Whalen. An irresponsible lout, but he does know horses. I think they talk to him. Then there is my cousin, dear, dear Judith, who was a favorite of my father's. He and Mother brought her up, along with me. I don't hate her. I just don't like her attitude on life. Her obvious greed, sometimes her snide insults. So there you have them. Len, Judith, Gordon, and my mother. I can't stand them. I wonder if you can. I wonder if I'm taking you into something so disagreeable it will affect our love."

"Alex, that is not possible. Nothing could do that."

"Then I ask you for the second time, will you marry me?"

"Yes. You and your family."

"Thank God," he said fervently. "I'll write and tell them I'm going to be delayed. They'll be pleased with that news. I'll tell them about you and that I intend to marry you. At once— Or no, no, I'll tell them I'm going to marry you in a month. That gives me an excuse to stay here in New York. But, Amy, my love, will you marry me tomorrow? In the next couple of days? As soon as you can? I don't want to wait, and I don't want to take you back to the farm now. We've too much to enjoy being alone."

"I will marry you as quickly as it can be arranged," I said. "There is nothing I want more than that. Because I'm afraid this is a dream and I'll wake up."

"I know what you mean. I'll make the arrangements in the morning. Now let's not talk for a while. Just let me hold you close to me and let me go on dreaming, since I, too, know it's not a dream."

We were married two days later. Marion was my bridesmaid and an assistant manager was Alex's best man. We saw no point in traveling on a honeymoon, when New York offered far more than we'd find anywhere else.

Alex was as wonderful a husband as he was a lover. We seemed to blend personalities and likes and dislikes so perfectly. He was kind and considerate, he made no unseemly demands, partly because it was so unnecessary. We loved each other and we loved our lovemaking. I was never so happy, never so content.

He wrote home and told them of the impending marriage, which of course had already taken place. Soon after that, he gave me a large brown envelope, sealed.

"Keep this," he said. "If the time comes that you'll have to open it, you'll know when."

I had a good idea what the envelope contained. I put it away. He insisted I buy clothes . . . more clothes than I thought it possible to own. Jewelry he selected himself, and from Cartier's and Tiffany's. His selection was amazingly tasteful.

He was an early riser, and while I lazily lay abed, he would go riding in the park. And I gave him my promise that when we went home to Greenlawn, I would learn how to ride. I was even eager for it.

We'd been married almost one month. The day was drawing near when it would be time to go home and there I'd meet those relatives. I didn't dread the ordeal. I hoped I would be accepted by them and not feel that I was an unwanted stranger.

This morning Alex went out before daylight, for a last ride in the park. I knew when he came back he'd be famished, so I arose at an early hour and ordered breakfast to be sent up after he came through the lobby. We'd heard from his mother, a warm letter, a happy one, showing that she approved. Judith wrote also, very briefly, a letter written because it was necessary to tell us that a suite of rooms was being made ready for our return. It was as cold and impersonal as some of the business letters I typed.

They came about ten o'clock, after I spent all that time worrying about him. They told me he had suffered a riding accident and he was in the hospital. That it had taken some time to identify him so I could be notified.

I learned during the ride to the hospital that he'd apparently been thrown. The horse, with a broken leg, was found nearby. Alex was unconscious. They didn't know how serious his condition was.

And so it came about that I was going to Greenlawn, a little earlier than scheduled. Alex was returning as well, but in a baggage car four cars behind my pullman.

He was going home in his coffin.

2

My first glimpse of Greenlawn Farm was from the back seat of a carriage riding behind the black hearse with its four black plumed horses as I accompanied Alex's body from the railway station.

Oddly, nobody met me except for the hearse and the carriage driver, an inscrutable Negro who said nothing and, until he called out to the horses, left me with the impression he was unable to speak. Apparently he had been ordered not to talk to me. I took this lack of courtesy on the part of Alex's family as a deliberate snub, meant to intimidate me so they'd be rid of me as soon as possible. I was not in a friendly frame of mind as the two-vehicle cortege drew up before the mansion.

It was a large brick house. The center of the building was two stories high and extended quite far back. On each side of it were two wings of one story. I learned quickly enough that one wing was devoted to a large kitchen and an even larger dining room while the wing to the right was devoted to a single enormous room that doubled as a drawing room and ballroom.

The front of the house was adorned by a plantation-type porch with eight fifteen-foot Grecian pillars. Between the pillars were large matched urns filled with flowers. It was a beautiful house, surrounded by more than five hundred acres of woodland, fields, gardens. There were also paddocks, stables, and even a racetrack.

None of this made much of an impression on me. Waiting before the veranda stood four Negroes in dark-blue uniforms. They immediately formed two lines behind the hearse, opened the door, and removed the coffin, which they raised to their shoulders and carried into the house.

This ritual completed, two men emerged. From the rather vivid descriptions Alex had given me I recognized the tall thin one as Len Whalen, Alex's uncle. The other man, powerfully built, heavy, but with little fat, was certainly Alex's stepfather. They looked most solemn as they waited for me to approach them.

"I am Alex's uncle and this is his stepfather," Len Whalen said. "And you are Miss Amy Wilton?"

They had no idea Alex and I had married and I wasn't about to inform them of that fact just yet. I wanted to find out what kind of people they were. True, Alex had warned me about them, but I wished to see for myself.

"Yes," I replied. "I've brought Alex home."

"You will no doubt stay for the funeral?" Gordon Holbert asked.

"You are indeed welcome," Len added. "Thank you for making this sad journey."

I didn't mind Len. He had a soft, gentle voice. But Gordon's was harsh, irritating, and impatient. He would have liked me to get aboard the carriage and go straight back to New York.

"I wish to stay," I said. "I'm sure Alex would have wanted that."

"Come in," Len invited. He stepped aside for me to precede him. In the reception hall Alex's mother waited for me and his cousin Judith stood at her side. I instantly liked Veronica Holbert and I quite automatically went to embrace her and kiss her cheek. She couldn't have been more than fifty, but she looked much older. Like someone beset with troubles for so many years they had been indelibly imprinted upon her otherwise quite pretty face.

Judith, on the other hand, was slender, with light-brown hair severely pulled back, and a rigid spine indicating too much pride and self-esteem. She extended her hand, but formally and coldly, murmuring something I didn't quite catch because Len was speaking.

"I think we should put Miss Wilton up in the green room, don't you?"

"I'm sure she'd prefer the room Alex loved so well," Gordon said.

"But that's Alex's bedroom," Veronica objected mildly. "Perhaps she wouldn't wish to—"

"My dear Veronica, Miss Wilton does not appear to me as a squeamish, silly girl. She will have Alex's room."

That settled, a servant went out to the carriage for my baggage. I had no chance to look about sufficiently to appreciate the furnishings, for I was promptly whisked upstairs by means of a lovely, marble staircase along a wall where paintings of horses hung with little space between them. At the top was a landing looking down at the reception hall, and from where the two great chandeliers could be seen at their best advantage. With the front door still open, they sparkled like so many massive diamonds in the sunlit hall.

Judith led the way with Alex's mother behind me, but at the upstairs landing she hesitated and then stopped, turning into what must have been her own room. Judith continued to lead the way.

Alex's rooms were large. One a fair-sized parlor, the other a spacious bedroom with a bath. My bags were already there. Obviously the servants had heard Gordon tell me where I was going to sleep.

"The funeral is tomorrow afternoon," Judith said. "There will be a great many people. I note that you are not wearing black. It is customary here to wear mourning clothes. Perhaps in New York it is not necessary, but we are provincial folks here and we abide by the rules."

"I have a black dress in my luggage," I assured her.

"Alex will be in the music room, just off the drawing room. Supper is at eight. We often dress, but not tonight. We are all too affected by Alex's untimely death. It's said he was thrown by a horse."

"That is what I was informed," I said.

"Miss Wilton, Alex wrote us that you are a bookkeeper at the hotel where he stayed. I do hope you have not jeopardized your job by taking all this time off."

"No," I said. "I am not concerned with my job, thank you."

"I'm glad. Well, I'll leave you to unpack. Come down whenever you wish."

"Thank you," I said.

She closed the door after her and I sat down wearily on the edge of the bed. I wondered what I had gotten myself into with this strange, lofty, cold family. No wonder Alex disliked them. I made up my mind then not to tell them Alex and I were already married. That could come later.

I cleaned up after the long train ride, hung up my clothes, the few I'd brought. The black dress was simple, selected by Marion at the dress shop in the hotel and altered so that it fit perfectly. Not that it made much difference to me, for I was not here to exhibit a style show but to walk behind my husband to his grave. In my handbag was the rather large, sealed, and now-folded envelope Alex had given me. I had not broken the seal.

When I went downstairs, no one seemed to be about, though I could hear voices coming from the kitchen. No visitors had yet arrived. I wondered how Alex's people were going to explain me.

Then I gave no further thought to the family, for I walked into the music room, where a catafalque had been prepared on which Alex's casket rested. I stood beside it and prayed for him. He looked so young. There wasn't a mark on his face, no evidence of what he'd gone through.

I was aware that someone stood beside me. I raised my head. Alex's mother reached out a hand to grasp mine while we shared our sorrow.

"It has happened too often," she said. "Much too often."

"Alex told me about his brothers. I know they must have been like Alex, and I know your grief is threefold that of mine. I loved Alex. I never loved a man before, but I knew I loved him the moment we met."

"Alex would have been like that," she said. "He'd know instantly if he was in love. He made up his mind quickly, and I'm very sure that when he made it up about you, he was using his very best judgment. You are so pretty, my dear. No—you're beautiful. And there is something about you I admire, whether I know what it is or not. Perhaps because you seem so straightforward. I like that. Mainly because I'm not like that at all."

"I'm sure you are, Mrs. Holbert," I said. "Alex talked often about you. He loved you very much."

"All my sons did," she said quietly.

Gordon interrupted any further conversation. "The Arnolds are here," he said. "We might as well begin."

I stepped aside with Alex's mother. Four people entered, two quite elderly. They stood by the coffin and the older woman wept openly. They came to us and took Veronica's hand. No one even so much as nodded to me.

It was like that the rest of the afternoon and evening. I'd not taken note of any farms or dwellings close by and some of these people must have come from a distance. I judged no less than thirty came, but no one introduced me. I realized then that I'd not been accepted by this family and that all they wished was that I would go away.

I had supper at the long table in the dining room; the food was excellent and served on china with sterling service. Little was said during the meal. I didn't feel like talking anyway. With Alex lying so short a distance away, I had no appetite. I ate because I wished to be sure I'd not be ill or faint next day.

I slept well. Alex was so close I could almost feel his presence all around me. If Gordon had hoped I'd be frightened in this room, he was much mistaken.

Alex's clothes were in the large closets, including riding habits, one with a scarlet coat that he had told me he wore at the fox hunts. His boots, brightly polished, were lined up. His possessions filled the bureau drawers. I wept when I was alone, but not so much in sorrow over his death as for what his life must have been living with these strange people.

I dressed in black in the morning. When I went downstairs, the house was already crowded with mourners. I slipped through the crowd. I saw Judith, but she paid no heed to me. Gordon was busily engaged in deep conversation with three men. Len was nowhere about. I made my way to the kitchen.

There I met Lena, a tall, willowy mulatto who quickly cleared a place for me at the breakfast table.

"They'd fire me if they heard this," she whispered,

"but I'm glad Mr. Alex met you and was happy, even if for only a short time. That said, I'll not mention it again. I can fix anything you like, Miss Amy."

"Thank you—mostly for what you said about Alex. We were happy. We had a few short weeks and I know he enjoyed them. I'm not very hungry. Anything will do."

"You got to eat, Miss Amy. It'll be a hard enough day. You can't go hungry."

She provided me with eggs, ham, the lightest biscuits I'd ever eaten, and coffee that was dark and strong. I had to admit I felt better.

"Lena, Alex didn't talk much about his brothers. What happened?"

"Merv died of pneumonia. I know that for a fact. Ben was thrown and killed."

"As Alex died?" I asked.

"It happened early in the morning. He was exercising a horse, one he had a lot of hope for. Nobody saw it happen. The jockey found him beside the track. It's like this family is cursed with bad luck."

"Neither Ben nor Merv was married?" I asked.

"They were both about to be. They died only a few days before the wedding was to take place. Merv's fiancée went off someplace and they ain't ever heard from her, far as I know. Ben's betrothed is here now. I saw her just for a second or two. Her name is Evelyn. She couldn't stand it here after Ben died."

"Isn't it odd how all three brothers died so early in life?"

"Yes, ma'am, sure was a strange thing. Funerals ain't no novelty around here."

Leonard, in a worn leather jacket, arrived to prevent any further conversation with Lena. "I've been looking for you," he said. "I want you to meet Evelyn. She was engaged to Alex's brother Ben."

"Thank you for such a delicious breakfast," I said to Lena. "I do wish to meet Ben's fiancée," I told Leonard.

He led me out of the kitchen and into the dining room, which was deserted. There he brought me to a halt. "I'm going to go perhaps further than I should, but I know how chilly your welcome has been and I shall try to make up for it. I want to be your friend, Amy, because I know how much Alex must have loved you, and I realize what a shock this must be. Enough that Alex is dead, but the way you were received is a shame."

"Tell me," I said, "why do they act this way?"

"For one simple reason, Amy. They are afraid you will attempt to put forward some kind of a claim to Alex's estate."

"And you, Leonard, what about you?"

"I've nothing. I want nothing. All I desire is to be around horses, to train and race them. If you do have any ideas, if Alex promised you anything, let it all go. You'll receive nothing. That has already been decided upon. They'll fight you all the way."

"Thank you for warning me," I said.

"Please don't let them know I told you this. Now with Alex dead, I have to rely on their generosity and it's not going to be easy taking their orders."

"Of course," I said. "I'll say nothing."

He led me to where a girl of about twenty-one or -two, stood by herself in a farther corner of the drawing room. A line had formed for the purpose of viewing the body, but apparently she either had paid her respects or did not intend to join the line.

Len said, "Evelyn, this is Amy. I told you about her."

Evelyn extended a hand and I took it warmly. She was a brunette with deep-brown eyes. Perhaps she was of Latin extraction, and she was appealing without being a raving beauty.

"Please," she said, "will you walk with me, Amy?"

"I was about to beg the same of you," I answered. "We are not too favorably accepted, are we?"

"You haven't yet felt the full brunt of their ostracism. No outsider is welcome here. The night after Ben's funeral they informed me very frankly that they did not wish me to stay. After I had breakfast next morning I discovered a servant had packed all my belongings, which Ben had brought and placed in the room we were to occupy after we were married."

"Don't you resent it?" I asked. "Ben was going to make you one of the family."

"Resent? No—I was happy to go. Even while Ben lived, they treated me as an outsider. I understand they told Merv's fiancée to leave soon after his funeral. She went, and we haven't heard from her since. I think they give her money."

"You live close by then?"

"About six miles south of here. My father has a small horse farm and raises tobacco. Ben and I knew each other since kindergarten. I don't think either of us questioned, for one moment, but that we would someday be married. I held off as long as I could. But I loved him so much that not even the prospect of living with this high and mighty family of his kept me from him. But I waited too long."

"We must talk more of this later," I said. "Privately, because there are very many questions I wish answered. I doubt I'd get any replies from Alex's stepfather, his uncle, or that strange cousin Judith. You know, if she would stop hating everyone, she would be a highly attractive girl. Hate shows on one's face, and not to one's advantage."

"Alex's mother is a darling, but she has little to

say about what goes on here. And she does drink too much at times."

"I've met her and you are quite right. She's as warm as Alex was, but so terribly shy. Perhaps that's why she drinks."

"With Gordon for a husband, anyone would. And Judith is no help. Leonard isn't so bad, except for the fact that his greed surmounts anything else in his life. Not for money, but for race horses. I think if he had a choice between ten million dollars and a winner at the Derby, he'd take the horse. In all his other dealings he's a fair and honest man, but when it comes to horses, he will gamble, cheat, and lie. I think he'd almost kill, to have his own way."

We talked for another half-hour before things were made ready. We paid one more visit to the casket. It was closed moments later. As it was carried from the house on the shoulders of the same four men, the family walked close behind. It was evident that neither Evelyn nor I was included in that smug family group. Veronica wept all the way to the family cemetery a quarter of a mile behind the house. The others held their heads very high. At that moment I had a rather good idea that I was going to bring them down considerably, and I would find it difficult not to relish great pleasure in doing so.

The service was not long. I stood close by the foot of the grave with Evelyn beside me. Once I glanced up and on a hilltop overlooking the green pasture and cemetery, I saw a man standing there, watching us. I couldn't make out what he looked like except that I felt sure he was quite young and very tall.

"Evelyn," I turned toward her, "who is that on the hill?"

She looked up. "Where?"

"On the slope . . ." There was no one there. "I

did see him. I wonder why he felt he had to attend the funeral from such a remote distance?"

"I don't know. I can't imagine who he might be. But understand, Amy, I didn't live here long enough to really get to know neighbors or friends. That's why I'm so ignored."

"Perhaps that will change one day," I said. "I suppose there will be a family meeting as soon as possible?"

"Tonight, without question, so they can make up their minds who gets what. Within ten minutes they'll be fighting over it. Hyenas fighting over a corpse. I hate them, Amy. That's an awful thing to say, but they are insufferable. And the boys were so unlike them."

"If Alex was an example, I know what you mean."

We walked back to the house and talked for a few minutes longer outside. Evelyn decided against going in, even to say good-bye to the family. I hated to see her go, for I sensed I was going to need a friend and ally before this night was finished.

Inside, the mourners were gradually taking their leave. By late afternoon the last of them had gone and Leonard closed the front door. I sat in the drawing room across from Veronica. Alex's mother was worn out by weeping and, quite likely, feeling as uncomfortable here as I did. She didn't come to my side when I sat down on a settee, hoping she would. Likely her husband wouldn't approve of it, so we sat apart from each other, sharing the same grief.

It was Judith who made the first advance. She stood before me, looking down her patrician nose. "When would you like us to have a carriage ready, Miss Wilton?"

"Would the morning be too soon?" I asked. I was deliberately baiting her, but I couldn't help it.

"Tomorrow will do," she said. "You can't get a train back to New York until then anyway, and you are welcome to remain here."

"But no longer," Gordon said. "We're not in a mood for visitors."

"Thank you," I said.

"I'm sorry we shall have to leave you alone, but amuse yourself as you wish," Judith said. "We have an important meeting with the family attorney. There are many things to be settled after a funeral, you know."

"I'm sure of it. May I attend?"

"Certainly not," she said promptly. "It is none of your affair."

"I was in love with Alex, he was in love with me," I said. "I believe that gives me a right to consider myself a small part of the family, if only for this one night."

Gordon heard the gist of the conversation and hastily came to Judith's side.

"She wishes to be part of the family," Judith said. "Isn't that amazing?"

"Why do you wish to sit in on the meeting?" Gordon asked me.

"Merely to observe."

"I think . . . yes. Yes, you may sit in. I've an idea you may believe you have some claim to something of Alex's. I don't know your motives, but by all means sit in so you can be very, very certain you have no claim upon any part of Alex's estate."

"What do you know of the estate?" Judith asked sharply.

"I know that this house, this land, and everything on it was owned by Alex alone. All of you are here by his sufferance."

"What a way to put it," Judith said. "We are here to run this farm and this house. Alex never stayed home long enough to have much to do with it. Gordon, I don't think she has any right to sit in on a private conference."

"Let her," Gordon said. "As I told you, she will then realize how hopeless it will be to ask anything of us simply because Alex was in love with her."

If Judith was about to continue her argument, it was upset by the arrival of a handsome, gray-haired man carrying a briefcase and an air of professionalism. I knew without asking that this was the family lawyer. They had certainly lost no time in summoning him.

Without a word to anyone, I made my way upstairs and there I removed the brown envelope from my handbag. I carried it downstairs and followed Leonard to the dining room, where the meeting was going to be held. I sat down, a few chairs away from the rest of them.

Leonard said, "Amy, I want you to meet Mr. Taber. He is our lawyer. Has been for many years."

"How do you do, Mr. Taber," I said.

He was at the head of the table, looking down at me. His smile warmed me. "I can well see how Alex fell in love with you, Miss Wilton. I wish I were younger."

"Thank you, sir," I said. "I have something here, given me by Alex weeks before his death. At that time he told me I would know when to open this envelope. I think that time is now. I believe this is what he meant. The envelope is sealed. I have no idea of its contents, but it should be examined now."

"We've got no time for that," Gordon said. "What goes on here does not concern you."

"Mr. Holbert," I said, "it does concern me. Please do not interrupt again."

"What are you driving at?" Gordon asked sharply as he came to his feet. "You've been acting like an upstart ever since you arrived. What are you trying to say?"

"Shut up and sit down!" My anger overcame my good sense.

Judith pointed a finger at me. "Kindly get out of this room and prepare to leave this house at once. You are impertinent, miss, and we have little use for that."

"Open the envelope, Mr. Taber," I said. "And put an end to these angry words."

"We are here to discuss the estate," Gordon insisted loudly. "That's all we are here for. But get on with it. Open the damned envelope."

Mr. Taber looked down the length of the table again. "I agree with you, Gordon, this young lady does seem to have something on her mind. I'm beginning to believe I know what it is."

"Alex and I were married several weeks ago," I said quietly.

"That's a damned lie," Gordon exploded. "He wrote and told us you would be married some time from now, I forget the date...."

"Please," I said, "the envelope may explain everything."

"Damn the envelope. I want it destroyed. We have no proof who wrote it and what it contains is immaterial...."

"Not if this young lady is Alex's legal wife," Mr. Taber said. He examined the envelope. "I note it is sealed with wax. Unbroken. If Miss Wilton—Mrs. Alex Paige—directs me to open the envelope, I shall do so."

"Please," I said.

He broke the seal before anyone else could object. At the foot of the table where he sat with a snifter of brandy, Leonard began laughing softly at first, and then almost uproariously despite the angry looks of Judith and Gordon.

Mr. Taber placed two pieces of paper on the table. "The first one," he said, "is a certified copy of a wedding certificate between Alex Paige and Amy Wilton. It is official, and there is no doubt but that they were married. Mrs. Amy Paige, welcome to the family."

I inclined my head just the slightest.

"The second document," Mr. Taber went on, "is a brief will, attested to and perfectly legal. In my opinion there is no possible way it can be broken. In it Alex leaves everything he owned, all his worldly goods and his love, to his wife. There is no provision in this will for anyone else. It clearly and boldly disinherits you, Gordon, you, Leonard, and you, Judith. It states that Veronica has means of her own, properly controlled by a trust fund so that Gordon cannot use it to his own purposes. In short, my friends, everything here belongs to Amy."

Nobody said a word, but presently Leonard began to laugh again and this time no one glared at him.

Judith said, "What do we do now?" in a most plaintive voice.

"I would say," Mr. Taber told them, "that you will have to make accommodations for whatever Amy wishes. There can be no compromise. Tomorrow, Amy, I shall have papers ready turning over to you all bank accounts and holdings. You are a wealthy young woman. I pray that you use his wealth as wisely as Alex would have wished."

"I give you my solemn oath on that," I said. "I will now say this. I did not know what was in the envelope, but I suspected it would be a will. It was Alex's wish that none of you share in his estate. He told me that several times."

"Now we have proof of it." Mr. Taber gathered

up his documents. "I will add a word of my own. I have never read or judged a will with so much satisfaction as I have with Alex's last testament. Good day, all."

He left quite abruptly. Leonard arose and came to my side. "What I have to say isn't worth much, but I'm glad it turned out this way. I ask of you, let me stay on the farm and care for the horses. I will work for very little money and I shall ask nothing more of you."

"Please remain," I told him. "Thank you for your kindness."

Leonard left us. I arose. Judith looked up at me. Gordon glared at me. Veronica kept her head bowed.

"What can I say?" Judith asked.

"I am not overly interested in whatever comes to your mind," I said. "I wish to go to my rooms now. We shall take up whatever business this change in your plans entails, in the morning. Good night."

Veronica raised her head. "Be kind, Amy. Be kind to us. We need kindness so."

"Will you come with me now?" I asked. "I would like to talk about Alex. I know so little, for I knew him such a short time."

"I will," she said. I went to her side and took her arm. It was so thin, and she leaned her weight against my arm as if she was sick or frail. We left the room. Judith had nothing more to say. Gordon buried his face in his hands. I almost felt sorry for him.

3

It seemed like a long, impossible dream when I awoke next morning. Overnight I'd become the sole owner of a very large, famous horse-breeding farm. I had no idea of the extent of the farm itself except that it was prosperous and extensive, but what cash assets or other property was involved, I had no knowledge. Attorney Taber would no doubt have all the answers.

And Alex's relatives, who had been so insultingly impatient that I clear out, were now living here at my tolerance. It had given me some satisfaction to see all their scheming evaporate, but I knew that I would have to do something for them. They'd lived on this farm most of their lives and had always considered it their home with no inkling of ever being dispossessed.

I didn't know what I would do about them. They were not very likable, except for Alex's mother. Of course, I would give no thought to making her leave. About Gordon and Judith I wasn't so sure. Leonard seemed far more friendly than the others, but I certainly had no more reason to trust him than Gordon and Judith, for I scarcely knew the man.

I dressed, took the time to write a letter to Marion at the hotel dress shop, asking her to arrange for all my possessions to be sent on. I gave her a full description of what had happened and I invited her down to visit for as long as she liked.

Then I made my way downstairs. I was accustomed to rising early so I could be at work by eight. It was now shortly after that time of the morning, but the dining-room table was not set and no one had come down. There also seemed to be a lack of servants. It occurred to me that I didn't even know how many there were.

When I pushed open the swinging door to the kitchen, I found them all assembled and waiting for me. Apparently they'd heard me leave my room and gathered to face their new mistress.

Lena introduced me to the upstairs maid and a stocky, very black, widely smiling woman named Marnie who was the housekeeper. A kitchen helper, a thin, seventeen-year-old young man who functioned as general handyman, and Prissy, the downstairs maid. I shook hands with each one.

"You have no doubt already heard that I am now the mistress of this house and the owner of the farm."

"We heered it, ma'am," Marnie said, "an' if it ain't sassy for us to say so, we sure ain't sorry."

"Thank you, all of you," I said. "I certainly do not intend to make any changes as to the running of the house. We shall discuss business matters in the next few days. I've no doubt you are all very good at your work."

"We better had be," Lena said. "Mr. Gordon, he ain't one to be pleased easy."

"We'll get along very well," I told them. "Lena, I would appreciate my breakfast now if you please. And when do the others come down?"

"Kinda late as a rule, ma'am. All 'cept Mr. Leonard. He's up long ago with the horses."

I made my way to the dining room, where a place

for me was quickly arranged. I ate another of Lena's fine breakfasts and decided that if this continued, I'd get as fat as a few of the horses I'd already seen down by the stables.

After breakfast I returned to Alex's room—my room now—and threw a shawl over my shoulders, for the early morning was quite crisp. I left the house and walked slowly to the cemetery, where I stood beside the freshly mounded, flower-covered grave of a man I'd loved so much and known such a short time. I said a prayer for him and mentally told him I would see that the work on the farm would be carried on as he would have liked it to be.

Then, to demonstrate that decision, I went to the main stable and discovered Leonard, in a tattered sweater, heavy trousers, and boots, at work currying a beautiful chestnut horse. He promptly laid aside the currycomb and took off his aged, sweat-stained hat.

" 'Morning, Miss Amy," he said.

"Good morning, Leonard. This is a beautiful animal."

"Getting him ready for you, Miss Amy. This is an Arab. Fine horse for a beginner. Thought about using a Morgan, and we got a beauty, but that breed produces small horses and this big mare is better for you, I'm sure. You'll find her reliable and easy-gaited. Got a fine saddle too."

"I don't think I'll try my first ride this morning," I said. The horse seemed so huge, but when I looked her over, I was fascinated by her dark almost-soulful eyes. I reached out and gently stroked her muzzle.

"She likes that," Leonard said. "I've got an idea you two are going to get along." He reached into his pocket and handed me two lumps of sugar. "This is a good way to make friends. Just put the sugar in the palm of your hand and she'll take it."

I held out my hand. The horse bent her proud head, soft lips brushed my palm, and the sugar lumps vanished.

"Thank you, Leonard," I said. "I know I'll be glad to learn riding on this animal."

"Call her Gracie, Miss Amy. Want me to show you around? We got some of the finest thoroughbreds anywhere. We won more races last year than any other stable in the state."

"Please let it wait," I said. "There is so much for me to try and catch up on, to understand...."

"Sure—Gracie won't mind." He caressed the horse's mane, and the animal rubbed its big head against his shoulder. There was no doubt that Leonard did have a way with horses.

"I want you to understand," I said, "that I wish you to stay and handle your work just as you always did. We can talk about shares later on. I don't want you to worry that you have to leave, or about money."

"Thank you," he said. "If I had to go, I've no idea of where I'd wind up. All I know is horses and I know the horses on this farm best. I've seen them bred, born, watched them grow, and I feel bad when they are sold."

"Your knowledge of the horses will be indispensible to me," I told him. "I intend to make this farm even better than Alex would have wished it to be, and I'll need a great deal of help."

"You have mine. Would I be out of place to ask what you're going to do about the others?"

"I don't know. I've not had time to think about it."

"Let them stay. They're a nasty pair, Gordon and Judith, but Veronica is no trouble. So far she's had nothing to say about anything that goes on here."

"I'll make up my mind quickly," I said. "Whatever

I decide will be for the good of the farm and I won't consider personalities or dislikes."

I walked about for another half-hour. Well behind the stables I saw the lush pastures where sleek, slender-legged, proud-looking horses were grazing. I had an idea these were the thoroughbreds. Behind that I came upon a racetrack. It looked huge to me, regulation size, though I couldn't be sure of that. As I moved up to the rail, a sleek horse with a gaudily dressed man in the racing saddle entered the track. He gave a whoop, slapped the horse smartly, and the animal began to run. I'd never seen anything like it. Twice the horse passed by the fence where I stood. I had no idea these animals could run so fast, or seem so graceful and strong.

As he passed for the second time the man in the saddle waved to me and I waved back. At first glance he'd seemed to be a small boy, but I had enough opportunity as he rode by to see that he was an adult, but small, lightly built, and I decided he must be a jockey.

I then made my way back to the mansion, and as I approached it, I became fascinated with the strange ways of fate. A month ago I worked in an office, getting experience in the operation of the newfangled typewriter. Then Alex came along and it all changed. Now I was here; all this was mine: the beautiful mansion, the wide, green fields, the stables, the horses—so many of them and so many kinds. It was going to take some time before I was fully acclimated to the fact that I was the owner of all this and I owed it to my dead husband to see that the farm he loved would be worthy of his memory. He'd told me a dozen times that he would like to pay more attention to the farm, to improve it and try to raise the best horses in the world, especially one who would win races and go on to real fame, which would give the farm a sure and smooth way to more successes.

They were waiting for me in the drawing room, seated around a small table with breakfast coffee on a tray. Veronica's eyes were still red and swollen from weeping, and she looked as if she'd slept little during the night. But Gordon was freshly shaven and smelled of bay rum. Judith, in a simple white linen dress, looked younger than she had last night. Her eyes were neither swollen nor red. They were ice-cold.

"We waited for you," she said. "It's time to talk."

"How nice of you," I said, equaling the chill in her voice. I sat down. Veronica indicated the silver coffeepot. I shook my head. I looked calmly from Gordon to Judith and waited for one of them to open the dialogue.

Judith said, "What do you intend doing?"

"I plan to remain here and operate the farm as if Alex were here."

"What do you know about horse breeding?" Gordon demanded.

"I can learn," I replied, keeping myself as unruffled as possible.

"The farm won't last a year under your direction," he said. "You need us to manage it for you."

"I see. Apparently this morning you agree with Attorney Taber that I am Alex's heir. His sole heir."

"It was unfair of him," Judith said sharply. "It was his way of getting even."

"If you think so," I said, "you are quite free to pack up and leave, Judith. I don't want anyone to stay here against her will." I looked at Gordon. "Or his," I added significantly.

"This has been my home since I was a child," Judith said, and her voice actually quavered. "I wouldn't know where to go. Or what to do."

Veronica, who sat close to me, laid a hand gently on my arm. "Please, my dear, don't be harsh with them."

"I want to point out one thing," Gordon said. "Veronica, Alex's mother, is my wife. I strongly doubt Alex ever considered forcing her to leave Greenlawn. And if I go, so does she."

He had me there, and well he knew it. However, I'd made up my mind quickly as we talked. I did need them. I barely knew what a well-bred horse looked like. I didn't know what they ate, how they were cared for, how long they lived. There were a thousand questions. Perhaps Leonard could answer most of them, but I also needed to know about money matters concerned with the sale of a horse, even how to go about making such a sale.

I thought also that whatever grief they had brought to Alex, they were well paid back now. I knew that it had never occurred to them that Alex would ever marry and, if he did, turn over every stick of property to his widow. They'd not even known we were married. Which gave me something more dire to think about.

Alex had written that we intended to be married. If these people knew about the will, or even guessed what it would be like, they'd have very good reason to kill Alex before he was married as his two brothers had died. The very idea was absurd, but yet it did bring little beads of perspiration along my forehead. I was so startled at the thought that I looked very sharply at both Gordon and Judith.

"I have already agreed that Leonard shall stay," I said. "There is no reason why either of you should have to leave the farm. What I do want from you is your full cooperation and your understanding of my ignorance of what goes on at a horse farm. I have no idea how you were recompensed for your services here. Whatever the arrangement was you may assume will continue."

"Thank you, dear," Veronica said softly.

Gordon arose. "You can depend on me, Amy. I'll continue to try to make this farm profitable and busy. When you have the time, I'll be glad to explain the financial situation here and show you an inventory and record of every animal we now own."

Judith arose slowly and stood before her chair for a moment. I knew how she felt. Ordinary courtesy, if not wisdom, demanded that she offer some kind of apology for the way I'd been received. She couldn't manage it, and she began to turn away.

I said, "Judith!"

She came to a halt and turned quickly.

"I would like to go riding with you some morning. I need someone to keep me from falling off my horse."

She drew a sharp breath and nodded curtly before she fled from the room. Gordon, too, left, and Veronica and I were alone.

"That was a splendid thing you did with Judith," Veronica said. "She's a strange girl. As haughty as our best thoroughbreds. Maybe that's what's the matter with her. She is a thoroughbred. This is not easy for her."

"Nor for me," I admitted. "Alex loved you very much. This feeling he had for you I shared with him then and I shall do my best to take his place in your heart."

"Thank you, my dear. I'm pleased you're here. I'm glad Alex left it all to you. I couldn't cope with it if he'd made me his heir, and they'd have taken advantage of me."

"Shall I trust them?" I asked bluntly.

She lowered her head to stare at her frail-looking

hands clasped on her lap. "I don't know. I . . . don't . . . know."

"Thank you. I'll take care."

"There is one thing you can be certain of." Veronica looked up with more confidence. "There is no one on this farm who will stand for a horse being injured in any way, nor will they permit a sale made to anyone who does not love horses and know their ways."

"I can believe that of Leonard," I said. "I'm happy Gordon and Judith are of the same mind. You look tired. Why don't you have an early nap? I'll see that you are not disturbed."

She nodded as she rose. "I am tired. I slept so little last night. Thank you, dear. I'm proud that my son met you—and married you."

She kissed me fondly on the cheek and then slowly left the room to climb the stairs. I watched her go up them, and she appeared to me to be older than Alex told me she was. If this was due to Gordon's behavior, I intended to do something about it. With these people I would be careful and wary, and I had made up my mind that I would tolerate no instance of treachery or dishonesty.

I had discovered that there was another room off the drawing room, and that was where Gordon had disappeared. I went there, opened the door to a fine, conservative, attractively furnished office with all dark wood, thick carpet underfoot, heavy draperies at the two cathedral windows.

Behind the desk, Gordon occupied a high-backed leather chair, but as I entered, he came to his feet, swung the chair in my direction, and bowed slightly.

"Welcome to the heart of the horse-breeding farm, Amy. This is where the big decisions are made. This is now your chair and your office."

"Sit down," I said. I favored one of the smaller

chairs facing the desk. "I've no desire to take over that much. What I wish to know now is something about the strange death of three brothers, all dead, two just before their marriage."

"What is there to tell? Unfortunate is all I can say about it."

"You can believe then that the three deaths were merely a coincidence?"

He seemed startled at the idea. "I never thought otherwise. Why should I? Do you have reasons to suspect there was something wrong?"

"Only in that it seems strange that three fine young men are dead. What of the fiancées they left? I've met Evelyn. I like her."

"Fine young woman," Gordon agreed. "Ruth is another thing."

"She is the girl Merv was to marry?"

"Yes, and a troublemaker. She has threatened all sorts of dire things if we do not continue to support her."

"I see. I shall talk to her soon. Now please begin my lessons in the breeding and training of horses. From the viewpoint of a financier."

Gordon relaxed. He produced ledgers of all sizes. They contained histories and a snapshot of each horse. On every entry was dutifully listed the history of the animal in fine detail. For two hours I sat with Gordon until the facts he presented to me began to make some sense, though I knew I had much more to learn before I understood all the facets of this business. It was interesting. I could see why Alex had loved it so. I felt grateful to Gordon for his efforts. He was a brilliant man, but there was a long way to go before I would trust him implicitly.

A week later I was even more impressed with Gordon's abilities. He had innovated a new way to sell horses by having photographs taken of them from all angles, not only for our records. By this method he had sold two dozen horses to a girls' school up north for a sum that actually startled me.

To back all that up he was now arranging to sell forty Morgans, those small, beautiful horses, to a boys' military academy in Boston, after having convinced the authorities there to augment the military training by adding a small cavalry unit with horses suitable for boys.

"I have to go to Boston soon to close this, but I'm . . . that is . . . we're getting a mighty fine price for this herd."

"You're doing very well," I admitted.

He condescended enough to say "Thank you," but I think he looked for more praise than I had given him. I didn't like the man—not yet, if ever. My trust in him had grown slightly, but I was not overwhelmed by it.

It did seem to me he was treating Veronica a little better. Lena had told me he was being more attentive to her, taking her for rides into the countryside, and refraining from bringing her the bourbon bottle she had been so accustomed to having at her slightest hint. I recalled that Alex told me his mother drank too much as a compensation for her husband's neglect, but that seemed to be no longer the case. I'd seen Veronica take a drink—several, in fact—but never to excess, and she seemed more cheerful.

A week had made a difference. I was certain about that except where it concerned Judith, who always ate her meals with us, but didn't say much. She did some of the bookkeeping, at which she seemed as expert as I used to be when I worked at the hotel. But mostly she remained in her room.

I was slowly getting an education in horses and the raising of them. Leonard, especially, took pains to teach me as much as he could. I still had not ventured to get aboard my own horse, idling its time away waiting until I was ready. Leonard teased me about it several times, but I hadn't made up my mind about riding. Not yet. What had happened to Alex was still too fresh in my memory.

This fine early-spring morning I went for my usual walk, and as customary, I wound up at the stables. But this morning, when I walked out from between two stable buildings, I came across Judith in what seemed to be intimate conversation with Carl Terrell, the jockey employed on the farm.

Judith saw me approaching first. She, surprisingly enough, came to meet me. "Good morning, Amy," she said. "Carl and I were just discussing how we could get you into a saddle for a ride."

I was astonished at this approach. "Well, I've been trying to get up the nerve..."

"Amy, if you are going to learn how to ride, it has to be now. This morning. Carl was about to saddle a horse for me. I suggest he prepare another for you and we'll take a slow ride along some safe trails. You have to learn sometime. After all, your business is dealing in horses. You should know how it feels to ride one."

I wasn't sure if I accepted that invitation because I did want to learn how to ride, or whether it was to exploit this sudden warmth from Judith. I wanted her to like me. That may have been a fault of mine. I wanted everyone to like me, no matter what their attitude may have been in the past.

"All right," I said. "I have a brand-new riding outfit I ordered from New York. I shall need time to change."

"I'll change too," Judith said. "You'll love riding when you get used to it."

We walked back toward the mansion while Carl

arranged to have the horses waiting when we returned. This was the first time I'd walked side by side with Judith. She was a rangy girl who took long steps I had to work hard to follow, and she bubbled over with enthusiasm for the coming ride.

"I never had much of a chance to ride with anyone. Leonard hasn't time; Gordon doesn't care about riding, as he considers it a waste of time. Veronica gave it up long ago. Carl is the only one I have ridden with and he's a bore."

"I hope I can fill in for him then," I said.

She looked directly at me as I matched her long strides. "I'm never a hypocrite, Amy. I hate you for marrying Alex. I hate you for taking over this farm. I will ride with you because I believe you should be taught how to handle a horse—and because I get so darned lonely."

"I'm sorry you don't like me," I said, somewhat taken aback by her outspoken ways. "Perhaps I can change that in time. For now, I admit I'm lonely too. Perhaps we need each other, so we might as well make the best of it."

"Well, we won't come to blows," she said with a very small smile. "But I'll bet your riding outfit is going to make mine look sick."

"Oh, yes," I said gaily, "I'm sure it will. Mine is the very latest style."

She looked my way with the first sign of good humor she had ever displayed to me. We both went upstairs to our own rooms.

Judith was ready long before I had changed into my brand-new riding habit. She came to my rooms while I was pulling on my riding boots. I looked up and wagged my head back and forth at the sight of her. "You mentioned that my riding habit would likely make yours look sick," I said. "How right you were."

BRIDAL BLACK

She wore slate-gray men's trousers, tucked into short boots, a man's checkered shirt open at the neck, an old, somewhat scruffy jacket, and all of this topped by a jockey cap in blue and silver.

When I put on my jacket I looked like a polished peacock in comparison. My trousers were tucked into high, polished boots. Under my scarlet riding jacket I wore a shirtwaist tight around the throat and a regulation derby topped it all off.

"If we were riding anywhere but around the estate, I'd never be seen within two miles of you," Judith complained.

I said, "Judith, you have just resolved a mystery that's been plaguing me ever since I met you."

"Me—a mystery?" she scoffed.

"In that outfit you have just revealed yourself. You're a tomboy! You're someone exactly suited to life on a horse farm, and your riding outfit becomes you far more than mine does me. I'm a tenderfoot. I don't know what riding is all about, and my outfit suggests it. Yours makes you look like you were born to ride, and I suspect you're as good as any man who ever sat saddle."

She smiled, this time a genuine one showing how pleased she was.

"If you grew up with three boys, you'd act like a tomboy too. On my part it was self-preservation. I consider your appraisal of my outfit a compliment. But honestly, there have been many times when I wished I was more ladylike. However, for this moment a tomboy predominates. I'll pick you up if you fall off the horse."

4

Carl had two horses saddled and ready. He indicated which was mine before he helped Judith onto the animal he had selected for her. Neither looked very much like the sleek horse Leonard had reserved for me. My experience, limited so far, did enable me to judge that we were being provided with two thoroughbreds.

I was about to comment on this when Leonard emerged from a stable leading the horse he had already assigned to me.

"This is your nag," he said. "You might as well get used to her first before you start riding these thunderbolts Carl got ready."

"Thank you," I said. "I'm sure I like the one you chose best. Now, how do I get on her back?"

I stood on the wrong side, so Leonard led me to the opposite side. There he made a stirrup of his hands. "Swing up there," he commanded. I lifted my foot and felt myself hoisted up and I managed to get a leg over the saddle.

"You look fine up there," Leonard commented. "Now I've told you how to handle a horse. I hope you remember it all."

So did I. I touched my heels lightly against the horse and suddenly I was in motion. I held on for dear life and I clumsily tried to match my precarious seat with the gait of the animal. But Leonard had

BRIDAL BLACK

chosen well. After a few more minutes I felt more comfortable, and then Judith rode up beside me, looking pleased that she could gloat over her superiority at riding.

"We'll just go for a trot across the fields," she called out. "After that, I'll take you on the track and show you some real riding."

"Believe me," I said, "I won't show you anything on a track. I can barely hang on at this speed."

Gradually I came to adjust to this, for me, novel way of travel. And after another brief period I began to enjoy it. My horse was steady, answered me instantly, and seemed quite content even if she had an inexperienced rider on her back.

We rode for about half an hour before Judith signaled me with a wave of her hand to follow. She headed for the racetrack. The entrance was not barred and she reached the track first. I rode up beside her. The horse she rode was doing a good deal of head tossing, like an animal impatient to get on with whatever her rider meant for her.

"Get up some speed," she told me. "Don't be afraid. That nag won't throw you and she needs a good workout. Just let her run and hang on."

I held my breath for a moment, wondering if I was being tricked into something I couldn't handle. But I was here, on the horse, and expected to be taught how to ride well. I dug my heels, the horse took off at a speed that made me gasp and hang on. Apparently this was what the animal wanted, a chance to run fast, to let out her speed and enjoy it.

I thought I was doing very well indeed and going about as fast as a horse could run. Until Judith came up from behind and passed me as if I stood still. She raced on, leaning forward, urging her horse to more and more speed. The animal responded and I knew it was a thoroughbred putting to shame the speed of the Arabian I rode.

Judith was a fine rider, but as she passed me again she seemed to be having some difficulty in keeping the horse away from the rail. The animal actually appeared to me as if it wished to brush off its rider.

I had a glimpse of Judith's face as she went by and I realized she was in some sort of real trouble. I could do nothing about it, except try to follow her. The horse she rode was deliberately trying to force her off its back by pushing her against the track rail at high speed.

Suddenly Judith threw herself to the right and tumbled off the horse onto the track. The horse kept going as if it led an important race and cared little if it had a rider on its back.

I rode up as fast as I could, turned my horse to block any chance of the riderless thoroughbred from trying to run over Judith as she lay in the dust of the track. I did this by instinct, I suppose, but when the thoroughbred came by, it shied away to the other side of the track. I knelt and raised Judith somewhat. I discovered her eyes were open and she seemed more stunned than hurt.

"That . . . that . . . damned fool!" she cried out angrily.

"Are you all right?" I asked. "You went down so hard."

She managed to sit up. "I'm not hurt, I think." She stretched her legs out. "But my pride aches. That damned Carl gave me a horse he knew was impossible to control and always tries to brush a rider off by running against the rail. I could have been hurt. . . ."

She suddenly began to cry. A most amazing thing for Judith. I put my arms around her. I held her close to me until her sobbing ceased.

BRIDAL BLACK

"Amy, I'm sorry," she said. "I'm a fool. More of a one than Carl. I've tried to fight you, but I can't do it any longer. I was mad because I felt cheated when the will was read. I hated you, but I'm sorry. I'm feeling a little crazy I guess."

"You're lonely," I said. "There's no one on this farm you can adjust to. I'm lonely too. I have been for a long time. The trouble is, we're too proud to admit it, even to ourselves."

I helped her up. She rubbed her thighs and moaned a little. "I'm going to be black and blue from head to foot in the morning."

"Just so nothing is broken," I tried to comfort her.

"You do care about me, don't you, Amy?"

"Of course I do. What a question! When I saw you fall off the horse, I was scared to death."

"I didn't fall off. I threw myself off, before that darned horse smashed me against the rail. Look at it now, standing as meek as some old plug. That horse is a menace. I couldn't even pull her up when she was running that way."

"Whatever made Carl saddle it up for you?"

"Carl has a streak of cruelty in him. He's won some very important races and it's gone to his head. Well, let's get out of here. Mind walking to the gate? I'll take your horse, round up that murder-bent stallion, and lead her back to the stables."

"Of course," I said. "I'm glad you didn't ask me to handle that chore."

"You'll learn. You did well, if you want to know my opinion. And the way you turned your horse to block the runner was something fine. You may have saved me some broken bones."

"I'm glad," I said.

She stepped a little closer to me. Her eyes looked straight into mine. "You're not trying to fool me?

You have every reason to hate me, to order me out of your life and off this farm."

"I'm not trying to fool anyone, Judith."

"Well, I like you. I never thought I'd admit it, but I'm glad you're here. I'll see you at the stables."

On the way, after I exited the racetrack, I walked beside one of the paddocks where a horse was rearing up, tossing its head, slamming its forelegs down in what seemed to be a massive rage. I looked again and let out a long breath. I was sure that was the horse Carl had saddled for me. I'd have been at least hurt, if not killed, riding that wild animal.

Leonard was seated on top of an old barrel, idly twirling a rope.

"Did you see what happened?" I asked.

"Why'd you think I brought out old Gracie?"

"Did Carl deliberately saddle two mean horses for Judith and me?"

"No, I can't say he did it on purpose, but I can say he sure should have known better. I wasn't worried about Judith. She's a good rider and knows what to do, but the nag Carl saddled up for you is a real stinker."

"I intend to see what Carl has to say about this," I said angrily.

"Go easy on him, Miss Amy. He's one of the finest jocks in the state, and they're hard to come by. We'll be racing this spring and we'll need him."

"I'll think it over," I said, not appeased, but warned by someone who knew more than I did about racing. "He could have killed Judith."

"Not likely, but he sure could have killed you. You ride again, for now use Gracie and no other horse."

I walked with Judith toward the big house. Now that our mutual animosity was finished with, we

BRIDAL BLACK 51

were as friendly as devoted sisters. We even matched our steps as we walked.

"Judith," I asked, "why would Carl want to injure us?"

"I don't know about you. Hurting you wouldn't gain him anything, but it's probably his pride. He thinks I should swoon in his presence. He wanted to teach me a lesson and warn me I should pay more attention to him."

"He doesn't belong on this farm," I said.

"Honestly, Amy, you need him whether you know it or not. A great deal depends on the jockey during a race, and Carl is one of the very best. I'd think twice before I did anything about him."

"That's what Leonard said. I suppose you two know best, but if he ever tries this again, I'll send him packing."

"I'm glad it happened," Judith said. "It woke me up. I've always been like that. I hate too much and I'm wrong most of the time. It takes a bang on the head . . . or elsewhere," she said with a grin, "to wake me up. Let me help you, Amy. This is not an easy place to operate. I can teach you many things—and learn from you as well."

"Judith," I said, "I have no intention of doing anything about you except pray you will stay here, because I need you too. There's so much I wish to know."

"Just ask," she said.

"Let's have tea," I suggested, "and I certainly will ask. We'll change first. I'm afraid you didn't do your riding outfit any good by that tumble."

Later she joined me in the drawing room, where Lena had already provided tea and some of her delectable cookies. Judith looked fresh and quite lovely in a simple dress of blue linen. She'd tied a blue and silver ribbon in her hair. I'd already surmised those were the racing colors of the farm.

I poured and handed her the cup and saucer. "I want to know about Alex's brothers," I said. "About the way they died. Gordon was very evasive when I asked him the same question."

"Why do you ask me this question?"

"Because I think it more than strange that two brothers should die just before they were to marry and the third died after he was married, but the marriage was kept a secret and no one knew that he was no longer single."

"Do you suspect that their deaths were not accidental?"

"I don't know if I suspect anything, but I'd like to know how three deaths happened."

"Merv died first—a year and a half ago. He was the oldest. He and Ruth Crandall were engaged. Now I told you before that I'm a girl who can really hate. I was woefully wrong about you, but not about Ruth. She is a vindictive, narrow-minded girl who feels she was cheated out of the good life Merv offered her. How he came to be involved with such a person I can't imagine, but he did fall in love with her. After the funeral she stormed out hurling dire threats at all of us, and vowing she'd get back at Greenlawn Farm some way or other."

"What about the way Merv died?" I asked.

"I can well imagine you were told he died of pneumonia."

"Yes, I've been told that. It's not an unusual way to die and I cannot make myself believe a murder could be committed by giving someone pneumonia."

"He died a week after he was thrown from a horse," Judith said quietly. "That sort of changes things."

"And Ben died after being thrown," I said.

BRIDAL BLACK

"So was Alex. All three died by what seems to have been accidents. I've thought about that many a time."

"Can you think of anyone who would do such a thing?" I asked.

"That's not an easy question to answer, Amy. Gordon might be capable of it, but why should he go to such extremes? He's married to Veronica, and that means he's married to the farm as well. Leonard is the most unambitious man I've ever known. If he had this farm, he wouldn't know what to do with it. As for me . . ."

"I don't suspect you in any way," I said. "Besides, this is all conjecture. It is possible three deaths could happen like that. I don't intend to make an issue of it. On a horse farm everyone does a lot of riding. There are bound to be accidents."

"Amy, do you have any living relatives?"

"No," I said. "There's no one."

"Then who would you leave this farm to if . . . you were also thrown? You have no one, as you say. Even if you made a will disinheriting all of us, all Alex's people, it would be very hard to make it legal. If you died, the farm would go to us no matter how hard you tried to make that impossible."

I finished my tea and set the cup down. "We're both talking nonsense, and if we go on with it, we'll begin suspecting everyone."

"I already have," Judith said quietly.

"What do you mean by that?" I asked with a slowly growing uneasiness.

"If you had ridden the horse Carl saddled up for you, I hate to think what would have happened."

I brought a hand to my lips in a gesture of sudden enlightment and fear. "I thought he did that out of spite, to teach me a lesson."

"Maybe he did. No one can be sure of our Carl's

motives. But I'd watch myself, Amy. I'd be very careful. If there's nothing to all this idle chatter of ours, still nothing is lost by being wary. If there is some substance to it, you'd be very wise not to take any chances."

"Thank you for warning me," I said. "But I must say it all seems so impossible."

"Three deaths under similar circumstances are what makes it possible, Amy. And there is one other."

She frowned thoughtfully, almost as if she didn't wish to go on, but felt she must.

"Another person we must suspect of having something to do with those deaths?" I asked.

"The Cumberland Stakes. You know about that race?"

"Not very much, I'm afraid. I know it's held right across the border in Kentucky...."

"It is the most prestigious race in the country, I'd say. The winner takes in a small fortune. The winning horse makes another fortune on a breeding farm like this. Our farm won, and lucky we were it did, because we were on the verge of bankruptcy after a series of bad-luck incidents. We won with Valiant, a great horse, but we wouldn't have won if Jess Foster's Boots hadn't broken a leg two days before the race. Jess claims we were responsible and he came here with fire—no, murder—in his eyes. There was an awful row before he left."

"Do you believe Jess Foster could have somehow been responsible for three murders? Assuming they were murders."

"No! Everyone else believes it, but I do not. Jess is a good man. A fine man. I've known him most of my life. He has a farm three miles north of here. Not as large a farm as ours, but of a size that could be very profitable, especially if he had won that race. As it is, he and his mother are hanging on by the skin of their teeth, as the saying goes. Still, I would never accuse Jess of anything evil."

"Do the others? Gordon, Len, everyone?"

"Yes, there has been talk."

"But not from you?"

"No, I would never say an unkind word about Jess."

"Perhaps that would be because you're in love with him?"

She promptly gave herself away by the reddening of her cheeks, even while she denied it. "Of course not, Amy. I like him, he's a fine man...."

"All right, Judith," I said with a light laugh. "You don't love him. You only admire him."

"Mind your own business," she said in sudden dismay.

"I'm sorry, Judith. But you do make it so obvious."

She laughed then. "I guess you're right. Trouble is, I don't know how he feels about me. I'm not exactly the most charming girl in the world. I make up my mind too fast. Len says I shoot from the hip. Oh, what's the use in talking like this anyway? I'm going up and see how Veronica is. We do have to watch her, you know."

"Yes, I know. Alex warned me. But I haven't seen her under the influence of drink since I got here."

"She's on her best behavior. It won't last. It never has. She doesn't get around enough. She stays by herself too much. She did have a very happy marriage, you know, and being married to Gordon is different. She should have stayed a widow."

"Judith, if Veronica doesn't get around much, why can't we bring folks here? Why can't we have a soiree? A big dinner and ball? Invite everyone around."

"It wouldn't work," Judith said. "Veronica

wouldn't stand for it. You'd need a mighty good reason for such a ball if you wanted her to attend."

"I see. Well, it was an idea. Perhaps I'll think of something."

Judith left me then, and I remained in the drawing room to enjoy another cup of tea, even if it was almost cold. A dinner and ball would help Veronica immensely, I felt sure. She was living inside a shell, an armor protecting her lost love, and she needed to come out of it. If I could change her, I'd repay Alex's memory a substantial amount. I tried to think of some reason for holding such an event. I couldn't very well give it in my honor. I doubted that, in her present mood and sorrow, Veronica would sponsor it. But if I could bring in someone . . . a friend. A guest. But I had no close friends, except for Marion, who had helped me with the loan of that dress. I decided to think it over. She might be the solution to the problem and I'd be repaying her kindness to me at the same time.

I spent the rest of the day in the office with Gordon while he explained his system of bookkeeping to me. As I was quite familiar with the subject, it didn't take me long to determine that Greenlawn Farm was not in the best financial condition.

"But coming along," Gordon declared confidently. "I'll be in Boston in a few days and conclude the deal I already told you about. That will bring in expense money at least."

"And after the expense money?" I asked dryly. Gordon was being too suave for me. I sensed something wrong.

"My dear Amy, the Cumberland will be run in a few weeks and we are entering the same horse that won before. Valiant—that's his name—outran anything on the track and will again, for Len has kept that horse in tip-top shape. The purse hasn't been determined yet, but it will surely put Greenlawn in the black for years to come. Our horse cannot lose."

"I can't argue that point," I told him, "because of my ignorance of horse racing. I shall have to depend on you."

"Believe me, the race is as good as won," he declared.

"I understand Jess Foster had a horse that might have won."

"Quite right. It was entirely possible, for that was a great horse. Jeff is running another this year, but against Valiant he has no chance. None!"

"When you return from Boston you will have to explain all this in more detail," I said.

"Amy, have you seen the statue of Valiant? Our winning horse?"

"I've seen no statue of a horse. I never heard of it before."

"It's in one of the barns. It was completed only a short time ago. The cost was—well, it didn't do our bank account any good."

"Then why the statue?" I asked.

"It will be placed at Cumberland in honor of Valiant and this farm. That's very important for sales of our horses. An honor, and a profitable one."

"If you assure me of that, then I must accept it," I said.

I went to my rooms and straightened out a few things, though there was little for me to do. The upstairs maid was very efficient. I rested until supper, and afterward we all sat around in the drawing room while Len and Gordon told stories of past races and famous horses. It was interesting, but too much of a good thing. Perhaps, I thought, Judith and I would have preferred to talk of gowns and New York and Philadelphia, and Richmond. Veronica had little to say and retired early.

I read for a time in bed, and when I blew out the lamp, I was tired. I went directly to sleep and very soon I thought I was dreaming of one of those races Len was so eager to talk about. I awoke and it wasn't a dream. At least I didn't think so. In the distance, faintly, though loudly enough to have awakened me, I heard the sound of a horse running very fast.

A horse on the racetrack at this hour? It was twenty minutes after one. It seemed impossible. Little that I knew of horses, it did seem odd one would be exercised at this unseemly hour. I was just curious enough to get out of bed, dress quickly, and make my way out of the house to hurry down to the racetrack.

On the way I saw or heard nothing. All was in darkness: the area around the stables, the cottages where the help lived. I looked back at the big house, and only a faint light shone in the window of my room and nowhere else.

I reached the track. It was deserted. Yet I was sure I'd heard those hoofbeats and they had to be accounted for. I prowled around until I was satisfied that no one was abroad. Now and then a horse would whinny softly, as if reluctant to break the stillness. I gave up and went back to bed. In the morning I asked Judith if she had heard anything, but she shrugged and said no. So did Gordon. I went no further with any questions.

I returned to my rooms and changed into my riding outfit. Judith was in her room and I gave her no invitation to ride with me. I had a special project in mind this morning, and I didn't want her to influence it in any way. This was something for me alone to do. I wanted to hear Jess Foster's side of the story.

Leonard ordered my horse saddled, and while we waited, I asked him about Valiant and the statue.

"Well, now," he said amiably, "I should have

shown you the statue long before now. Come along. It's down a piece, at the large white barn. We don't keep anything else in there. And we're not advertising the fact we had a statue made. Gordon wants to surprise the officials at Cumberland."

He opened the double doors of the large shed and there stood as lifelike a statue as I'd ever seen. I expected the back muscles to ripple and the horse to raise its head even higher.

"What a beautiful piece of work," I exclaimed. "I can see it must have cost the fortune Gordon said it did."

"He talked about that, eh? Surprised me he'd spend that much, but he did. Now would you like to see the real horse?"

Naturally I was very curious, and he led me to a pasture where the animal grazed. There were no other horses near it. I leaned against the fence and admired the living animal more than I had the statue. Truly this was a fine-looking animal. A chestnut color with white markings and white legs.

"That," Leonard said with great pride, "is a thoroughbred. The strain was evolved many years ago. It came from a mixture of Arab horses for speed and stamina, from the Barb horses for length, and from Turks for height. The combination has produced the best race horses of all time. Valiant is pure bred and worth in gold almost as much as he weighs."

"I am impressed," I admitted. "But if Valiant is such a fine animal, Jess Foster's horse must have been even greater, according to Gordon. He told me Jess Foster's entry might have won."

Leonard nodded. "It was a bad accident for Jess. But a lucky one for us. I believe his horse might have won, though Valiant would have given him a mighty good race. When the Foster entry was scratched, there wasn't another horse could even come close to Valiant."

"Tell me, what is Jess Foster like?"

"Oh, well, he's a nice-enough young man, I guess. At the time his horse was lost he was on the verge of coming to call on us with a shotgun, he was that angry. Right out loud he said he suspected we had something to do with the accident his horse suffered. Of course we didn't, and he simmered down after a while. His farm is doing tolerably well. We usually outbid him on sales. Lives with his mother. They don't socialize much."

"Thank you," I said. "I'll go riding now. You will notice I'm going alone. I need to gain more confidence and not have anybody to lean on."

"It's a good idea, Amy. I'm all for it."

I rode, somewhat nervously, for being alone during the ride was a new experience for me. This time I had to trust the horse rather than a riding companion like Judith.

Finding the Foster place was simple, for there was only one road and the farm was close to it. I turned down the road, and as I approached the house, a woman came out to stand on the veranda and watch me ride up.

The house was a two-story frame structure with a long veranda enhanced by pillars. I judged it to be about half the size of Greenlawn, but it was attractive and the grounds well-cared-for. Behind the house were the barns, stables, and outbuildings, all freshly painted. A large pasture provided ample space for the two dozen horses, all of which, even from this distance, looked like sleek, proud thoroughbreds.

I dismounted, somewhat clumsily, and walked up to the porch steps, where I looked up at the woman, who had never taken her eyes off me since I arrived.

She was surprisingly young, or seemed to be, for I judged this had to be Mrs. Foster. She was of average height with the figure of a girl. Her hair was a medium, soft brown, and her eyes were clearly light blue. She would have been an exceedingly handsome woman if it had not been for the set, firm, and angry lines of her mouth.

"Good morning," I said. "I am Amy Paige."

"I know who you are," she said coldly. "We don't get many newcomers around here. What do you want?"

"Only to meet you as a neighbor."

"If you intend this as a friendly visit, you may leave now, Mrs. Paige. I have no desire to become friendly with anyone connected with the Paige family."

I refused to be taken aback by such a cold, plain statement. "I'm sorry to hear you say that, Mrs. Foster. Perhaps I have made a mistake in coming here. Forgive me if that's the case, but you must understand I am new here, a total stranger with little knowledge of this area or its people. And an equally grave ignorance of horse farms. Or those who run them."

"You are a Paige, that is sufficient for me. I am very busy this morning. Good day, Mrs. Paige."

She turned about to walk the two or three steps to the door.

"Mrs. Foster," I said somewhat sharply, "you are making a mistake in judging me as a member of the Paige family. I am bearing that name only because I married Alex Paige. Whatever differences you may have with the rest of the family is no business of mine. I am not in the habit of making enemies. Nor of judging people too quickly. I came in the spirit of friendship and I leave with the same spirit, despite what you have said to me. You are mistaken about me, Mrs. Foster, and I hope to prove that one day soon."

She didn't turn back. I returned to my horse and managed to get into the saddle quite gracefully, I thought. I rode back toward the road, but when I had almost reached it, a rider came from a wooded area close by. Though I'd not seen Jess Foster up close before, I knew who he was. I pulled up.

We studied each other quite frankly. Jess was about Alex's age, somewhat taller, definitely more rugged-looking. He had his mother's eyes and a firm, set chin, but he was smiling and I'd not seen any sign of that on his mother's face.

"You are unwelcome here," he said. "I'm Jess Foster."

"Yes, I've been given to understand that, Mr. Foster."

"We do not like any member of the Paige family, Miss . . . Mrs. Paige."

"Then why did you see fit to come to my husband's funeral, even if you did stay some distance away?"

"You saw me, eh? Well, I wasn't trying to hide."

"You didn't answer my question. Why did you come?"

"I liked Alex."

"Thank you," I said. "I have been led to believe you hated every member of the Paige family."

"I didn't say that. My mother likely did, but I'm not quite that vindictive. Even though the situation called for it."

"Good day, Mr. Foster," I said.

"Hold on now. I have no reason to dislike or distrust you. Don't you judge me by the way my mother acted."

I relaxed somewhat. "Thank you. I'm glad to hear

you say so. Will you tell me, please, just what makes your mother that angry at the Paige family?"

"They haven't told you?"

"They only said your horse was . . . there's a word that means a horse was removed from the race. . . ."

"Our horse was scratched. Because it was dead. I had to shoot it."

"I'm sorry, Mr. Foster. I don't know the circumstances."

"The jockey who now works on your farm took the horse over a jump. There was a bramble bush behind the jump and the horse landed on it and fell. The horse was badly injured. We would have won the Cumberland with that horse, Mrs. Paige."

"How can you blame us for what seems to have been an accident?"

"Mrs. Paige, a bramble bush is not a tumbleweed. It does not come loose and it is not blown about indiscriminately. If chance made one such bush to do this, it becomes unbelievable when four lodged in the same place."

"You say it was Carl Terrell who rode your horse over the jump?"

"I fired him and Gordon promptly hired him to ride his horse in that year's Cumberland. He's been on your farm ever since."

"I see. This is a matter I intend to take up, Mr. Foster. Thank you for telling me how it happened. No one else has—so far."

"Then I'm glad we met. Good morning, Mrs. Paige."

"Just a moment," I said sharply. "I'm told losing that horse created very bad financial problems for you. Looking at your farm from this point, it seems to be doing very well."

"Mrs. Paige, what you see doing so well is practically owned by the banks. We exist by their generosity and faith. Are you satisfied now?"

"What are we fighting for?" I asked. "I've no animosity toward you. I cannot see why you hate me. The Paige family, perhaps, but I've not been here a month, we've never met before. Two strangers cannot possibly be angry at each other."

He smiled then, and it changed his appearance most pleasantly. He pushed his plantation-type straw hat to the back of his head. "Come to think about it, you're right. Very well, I don't dislike you. In fact, I enjoy seeing you and I envy Alex's good judgment. You may also know that I liked Alex. He, his brothers, and I grew up together. All the boys were fine men. It's the others I dislike and have reason not to trust."

"You are welcome at Greenlawn if you care to call," I said.

"Perhaps I'll do that," he said with a broad smile. "If only to see how Gordon and Leonard and Judith act. Thank you for the invitation."

"Good morning then," I said.

"I'm sorry about Alex. Very sorry. I considered him a dear friend."

I nodded briefly and touched my heels to the horse. I rode away without looking back, even though I knew very well that Jess Foster hadn't moved and was watching me.

I liked him. He was honest and outgoing. Reasonable too, for he listened to my side of it and even agreed with me that there should be no enmity between us. I thought then I would enjoy him as a friend whom I could consult when I found things beyond my ken. I needed someone besides Gordon and Leonard. And I didn't like the idea of Carl Terrell coming to work for our farm after he'd been obviously responsible for the death of the Foster entry in the Cumberland. I intended to know more about that episode.

5

I said nothing about meeting Jess Foster to anyone. I still didn't trust Gordon and there were times when I even wondered about Judith, despite her friendliness. I recalled, painfully, what my reception had been like when they had no idea I owned the farm.

Gordon returned from his Boston trip with a substantial order for Morgan horses, and he had made other contacts that spelled good profits for the farm. I couldn't fault him for laziness or indifference.

Judith, too, worked hard, helping to train some of the thoroughbreds, and even if she professed a dislike for Carl Terrell, she often rode with him.

Leonard concerned himself only with the horses. He worked early and late, missing more meals than those he attended. On the surface everything seemed wonderfully serene. We paid off some substantial bills, reduced the mortgage, and had a healthy bank account left over.

The only failure on the part of anyone was concerned with Veronica, Alex's mother. I suppose after the novelty of my arrival wore off, she reverted. Not that she drank to an excess as to be a nuisance, or even showed it by erratic behavior, but she drank heavily and spent most of her time in her suite. Gordon professed an inability to do anything with her, short of physical abuse. Judith didn't even try.

There was really nothing I could do. She listened to no one, and drinking became a refuge. From what, I wasn't certain.

I didn't see Jess Foster again for days. I didn't ride much. I did hope that he might come calling, as he'd hinted he might, but he never came. If I rode at all, it was close to the farm, for even after all those weeks I was still a novice at riding. Quite likely I would never be very good at it.

I did plan a lavish dinner and ball for May. The Cumberland Stakes would be held about mid-May and I felt that was a good time to bring all racing enthusiasts together. Gordon approved the idea wholeheartedly. Judith talked of nothing else. Leonard was oblivious to the whole thing. Veronica had no comments, but I had an idea she did not approve, mostly for personal reasons.

Judith and I went off to Richmond twice and to Roanoke somewhat oftener, for it was not too far away and had good dress shops and milliners, though nothing to compare with New York stores.

There was a certain excitement as we approached May and early-spring flowers began to show their heads. All talk concerned the Cumberland. Preparations were already made to transfer the statue of Valiant to a place of honor at the track. Valiant himself was being carefully trained and timed often at the private track. To me it seemed incredible that a horse could run with such grace and speed. I also had to confess that Carl Terrell was one of the finest jockeys in the business, as Leonard often reminded me.

There was also much to do about the coming ball. I had written Marion and invited her down to stay as long as she liked. The ball would be given in her honor, as an old friend of mine. Judith and I planned to go to New York for our gowns and our dresses for the Cumberland.

Everything was too well handled, too smooth. I told myself it could not last. I thought about Jess Foster often and had to resist the temptation to ride over and visit him. His mother's dour attitude dissuaded me more than anything else, including the impropriety of my calling upon him, a factor I would have disregarded easily with any encouragement.

It changed one night in April. Once again I was awakened by the sound of a horse being run over our private track. I'd forgotten the first episode, but when I hastily dressed to investigate, it came back to me. My watch indicated it was shortly after four in the morning, a thoroughly unseemly time for anyone to be running a horse. I drew a cape around my shoulders and quietly left the house. It was a moonlit night full of shadows, but the weather was at least mild.

I felt uneasy as I made my way down toward the track. I knew about fifteen or twenty minutes had elapsed since I was awakened and I was not surprised to find no sign of anyone abroad. Yet I knew I had heard the running of a race horse.

After an inspection of the track and a walk between the barns and through the stalls, I was on my way back to the house, completely bewildered by this strange business.

He stepped out from one of the stalls so quickly that I came to an abrupt halt and cried out in alarm.

"It's only me, Miss Amy," Carl Terrell said. "Couldn't sleep. I guess you couldn't either."

"On the contrary," I said, "I was fast asleep. How long have you been awake?"

"About an hour. I wandered around trying to get tired."

"About half an hour ago I'm sure I heard a horse running over the track. Did you hear anything?"

"Running horse? On the track? You got to be mistaken. I'd have heard that. Who'd run a horse at this hour?"

"I don't know, but that's what I heard and I don't think I'm mistaken."

He shook his head. "You got to be, Miss Amy. I been right here, walking around. Nobody brings a horse out at this time of night. What reason would anybody have to do that?"

"I don't know," I confessed. "This isn't the first time I heard a horse running in the middle of the night."

"I don't know about any other time, but not tonight. No, ma'am. I couldn't have missed that."

"Thank you," I said. "Good night."

He touched my arm. "Miss Amy, I bet I know what you heard. Come, I'll show you."

I followed him back to the stalls. He opened one of them, the last in a long line. Inside was a jet-black stallion, a huge horse that instantly began to move nervously when the door was opened. His head jerked up and he bared his teeth. Carl struck the animal across the nose. The horse tried to rear up, but the size of the stall prevented him from doing little more than bringing his hooves down as hard as he could while he screamed his rage at us. His hooves beat a savage tattoo on the floor of the stall.

Carl closed the door quickly, for that horse could easily have become a highly dangerous animal.

"That's what you must have heard," he said. "It's got to be that. This here nag has been vicious since the day he was foaled. Kicking and biting. Nobody can handle him—not even Len, and he sure got a way with horses. We been thinking about shooting this one, but he's got fine blood in him and more strength than most, so we use him for breeding, but you couldn't get me to lead that nag out of the stables. I think he hates everybody, especially me."

"The way you struck that animal," I said, "I can scarcely doubt it. I don't want you to do that again, with any horse. If the animal is mean and dangerous, he should be gotten rid of. I intend to speak to Leonard about that."

"Whatever you say, Miss Amy, but all I was trying to do was show you the noise you heard and thought was a horse running around the track. I remember now, the horse was pawing away at his stall a little while before you showed up."

"Thank you," I said, and I left him to hurry back to the house, for the night air was chilly. I was not, however, deceived by Carl's silly attempt to make me believe that the sound of a horse running around the track was only the pawing of some half-mad animal caged in a stall. There was no comparison in those sounds. I was still certain I had heard a horse being exercised and I believed Carl was lying to cover up what was really going on. As I knew little about horses and racetracks, I couldn't make a judgment as to the reason for trying to conceal the running of some mysterious horse. I also had a firm belief that if I inquired about it, no one would tell me the truth. If Carl was covering up, then everyone was in on this secret and determined to keep it from me.

I resented that, but it was typical of this family. Instead of querying them, I meant to ask Jess Foster about it. He would certainly know the answer and, perhaps, what to do about it.

I refrained from mentioning a word about what had happened during the night. No doubt Carl would soon inform everyone. I did trust Leonard, but I decided against talking to him about it too.

BRIDAL BLACK

And very soon after breakfast plans for the dance and dinner took precedence over everything else. This, according to Judith, would be perhaps the most important social event of the season, rivaling or exceeding all the other soirees that preceded the Cumberland. I agreed to make it the best possible affair because I realized that, as a newcomer, I had to develop friends and get into the swing of the social season, for it was obviously very important that I did.

Whatever was to be done was left to Judith and me. Veronica was in a helpless state, though trying hard to pull out of it. I sympathized with her and I guessed that there was some underlying reason why she tried to lose herself in an alcoholic stupor.

"I want to help her," I told Judith. "Alex loved her very much, and I can see that she would become a quite wonderful person if she could solve whatever problem worries her so."

"I don't think you're right about a problem," Judith said. "She's been drinking for a long time. She doesn't need a reason anymore, if there ever was one."

"There well could have been," I reminded her.

Judith gave me a sharp, inquiring look. "What are you talking about, Amy?"

"The violent deaths of three sons."

Judith nodded slowly. "She did begin drinking after Merv died."

"And the deaths of Ben and Alex must have been inducement enough to keep her drinking. It's as if she's trying to forget. To go into an alcoholic haze so she can't think."

"Well, I would not go so far as to believe that, but I agree, she was very much affected by the deaths of her sons. She had reason to be. They were fine young men with brilliant futures. I wish you hadn't set me thinking this way, Amy. It all comes back. I don't like it."

"It was something I had to say. I'm sorry it upset you, and I'll see if I can't remedy that. You know I want to bring a good friend of mine here to become our guest, in whose honor I will give the ball. It happens that she is an expert on style. So I suggest you and I go to New York as soon as we can and have her supervise the buying of our gowns."

Judith hugged me and grew wildly enthusiastic. "Amy, you're a wonder. I wouldn't have thought of that, and I wish so much to make an impression at the ball. It's a marvelous idea."

"Then you can begin packing. We won't be gone long. You'll like Marion, and you'll especially like what she knows about current fashions. It's her business, and her shop caters to some of the most socially prominent women, besides some ladies with a touch of royalty: baronesses, countesses, and the like."

"I'll adore her," Judith said. She hugged me again in her ecstasy. "And just think of the way we treated you when you first arrived. We thought you were looking for whatever you could get out of Alex's estate, and it turned out you got it all. I wish we could begin again because, really, I'm not a vindictive, greedy girl."

"You're forgiven," I said. "It was partly my fault because, while I wasn't positive, I did have an idea what was in the sealed envelope Alex gave me. I should have warned you, but I guess I was a bit upset too. Let's forget it."

"I know I will when we get to New York. I've been there before, of course, but never with someone who knows the city and has friends there. Especially friends who know about gowns and fashions."

BRIDAL BLACK

Leonard drove us all the way to Richmond to catch the train, and swore he'd be waiting for us if we sent him a telegram to tell him when we'd arrive. All during the journey to the station, Judith and I talked about plans for the ball, some of them ostentatious enough to cause Leonard to wag his head in disbelief of what he heard.

There was no slack in the same subjects as we rode the steam train north. We traveled by pullman, so the journey was comfortable and not too riddled with soot.

It gave me a great deal of pleasure to stay at the Plaza, where I'd spent so much time working under the pleasantest possible conditions. I had many friends there, and Judith and I were received like royalty. We were given one of the finest suites in the hotel, and Judith was very impressed with my standing at such a fancy place.

Our first visit, after we unpacked, was to Marion's exclusive shop in the lobby. She received me with a mixture of smiles and tears, and soon she and Judith were fine friends. She had received my letter about coming for a visit.

"I didn't answer because I wasn't sure I wanted to intrude. The way you described the ball, I felt I might be out of place there. I'm just a working girl and all that finery—"

"Nonsense," Judith said quickly. "The ball may be fancy—we're trying hard to make it so—but the people won't be. They're just like everybody else."

"With one exception," I said. "All they talk about is horses, racing, and the Cumberland Stakes. Besides, we have to have some reason for giving the ball, and so we are giving it in your honor."

"Oh, Amy, what an idea!"

"We have to have some reason," Judith added with a smile.

Marion gave in. "I'll have to go then, I suppose. Yes, of course I'll be there. I wanted to go. I was just a little scared, I guess."

"I'm sure you can turn the shop over to someone for a week, or ten days, or however long you like," I said.

"You'll earn your keep," Judith said. "We haven't decided on decorations or amusements, or even a menu. Truly, we need you, Marion. All you have to do in return is make us—all three of us—into the most beautiful women there and see to it every other female is jealous."

"It won't be a difficult task," Marion said. "Not with you two. I'm not going to comment on me. But let's begin by letting me show you a few of the latest styles. These are direct from Paris, and some from London. There's some good things coming out of England these days too."

Marion's success had enabled her to hire two clerks, and they took care of the shop while we stayed in the back room and tried on one gown after another. I wasn't quite as ambitious to be the best-dressed woman at the ball as Judith, so it didn't take me long to settle on a low-cut gown of primrose faille with a white satin sash.

Judith was torn between two gowns, finally. It was at Marion's suggestion that she selected a princess gown in dark-green chiffon velvet. The skirt was pressed to look like ribbing and it was all enhanced by a white lace collar and moderately puffed sleeves also of white lace.

While she tried to make up her mind, I excused myself so I might take the elevator to the nineteenth floor, where the offices and my old room were located and where I had so many old friends.

Even Hugo the elevator man greeted me with a big grin, though he seemed to grow quite serious as

BRIDAL BLACK 75

the lift made its stops to discharge other passengers. As we neared the top, he turned to me.

"You going to be long up here?"

"No," I said. "Only long enough to visit with my friends."

"Half an hour maybe?"

"All of that. Why do you ask?"

"No reason. Just no reason. Just making talk, I guess. You got lots of money now, ain't you?"

"I suppose I have to admit I'm not poor."

"I'm glad," he said. "Very glad."

We reached the top floor and I got out of the car, to be greeted by so many of my old friends. Work was suspended for a while as I told them of my sad fortune in losing Alex and my good fortune in finding myself the owner of a large horse farm. I described the place, told them how I was still learning how to ride. It was a pleasant hour before I left with a promise to look in again before I went back to Virginia.

Old Hugo was still running the elevator. The car started down, but while the board lit up, indicating he should have stopped for passengers at several of the floors, the car kept going, even passed the lobby floor. When it came to a stop in the basement, I was not only startled, I was more than a little annoyed.

"What in the world possessed you?" I said. "I've no reason to be brought to the basement, and you must have made a number of guests angry when you didn't stop."

"You willing to pay a friend of mine a little money if he got something important to tell you?"

"What's this all about?" I asked somewhat nervously.

"How your husband got killed," he said.

"What do you know about that?" My nervousness

vanished and its place was taken by anger, hope, and more than a little fear.

"Don't know nothing myself, but I got a friend who does. His name is Pauley. That's all you got to know. He's waiting just outside the elevator. I'll let you off and you can talk to him. I got to pick up guests before I get fired."

He opened the car door, left it open, and stepped out with me so he might call a man out of the shadows of the dismal basement. The man was very much like Hugo. A bit greedy, and it showed in his unctuous manner. Hugo stepped back into the elevator and it rose, leaving me alone with this stranger.

"Do you know something about the death of my husband?" I asked.

"Somethin', yes, I know somethin'."

"Well, what is it?" I realized he had stopped talking because he was looking for some kind of reward. I opened my handbag and gave him five dollars.

"Thankee kindly," he said. "Ain't much, but reckon it's enough to get started."

"Will you please tell me what you know? There'll be more if your story is truthful."

"It's truthful all right. I told Hugo about it, just makin' talk one day, an' he says he knowed you and your late husband. But what I got to say could get me in lots o' trouble, it ever gets out who I am, so I kept my mouth shut. I don't like cops with their damned brass buttons and nightsticks. They laid their clubs on me more'n once."

"Please, what do you know?" I pleaded.

"Well, the mornin' it happened, I was takin' a nap on one o' the park benches. One o' the benches kinda hid behind the bushes. I been there all night, you want to know the truth. I got no place to live. Ain't never had a place in my life. Money's hard to come by."

"I can take a hint," I said. "I'll see you get paid for what you know."

"Well, like I said, I was out o' sight when I heard this rider comin' along. He wasn't riding very fast, but then I heard him yell and the horse kinda screamed. I took a good look and I saw that somebody had fixed a rope across the ridin' trail an' he musta tripped the horse 'cause it was lyin' on its side an' this fine-lookin' gent was on the ground an' seemed like he couldn't move. Then somebody just walked up an' hit him across the head. I guess it was somethin' like a baseball bat. I ain't sure."

"This man . . . was it a man? Of course, it must have been. What did he look like?"

"Well, I told you it was very early, right after dawn, an' it was a gray kinda day, looked like rain, it did. I couldn't see very well. I jes' woke up too, you remember."

"You saw the man. Was he tall, or thin, short? What did he look like?"

"Ain't sure, miss. Jes' ain't sure. Kinda hard to see."

"I could call in the police."

"Wouldn't do no good. They can't make me say what I don't know."

"You want money, don't you?"

"Well, it might make my eyes open a little more," he said with a sly smile.

"How much?"

"Oh, I leave that up to you. An' like I said, I didn't get too fine a look at this gent, but if I saw him again . . ."

"If I paid you enough, would you come down to see me in Virginia?"

"Kinda like the idea," he said. "Yep, sure do. Never been in Virginia. Never been any place. I'll come down. You pay my fare. An' a little extra."

"I'll pay your fare, and if you can identify the man who killed my husband, I'll pay you well."

"All you got to do is let me know, ma'am. Sure would like to get on a steam train an' ride all the way to Virginia. Never been on a steam train."

"I'll send for you. Where can I reach you?"

"Well, that don't concern you rightly, ma'am. I can't read or write, so you just tell Hugo where I'm to go an' he'll get word to Pauley. That's me."

"You will hear from me in two weeks' time, no longer."

"An', ma'am, when you write to Hugo put in enough money so's I kin travel in style an' comfort. An' some extra—like I said. After I pick out the gent, you kin settle up. We kin come to terms on how much soon's I get there."

"As you wish. Don't fail me. It wouldn't be well for you if you did."

"Ain't goin' to fail, ma'am, 'cause I need the money real bad. Yes, ma'am, real bad."

I pushed the button for the elevator and it came down quite promptly. Meanwhile, the man I'd been talking to vanished in the gloom of the basement. I was beside myself with excitement, anger, and a renewal of my great sorrow. Alex had been murdered. That meant Merv and Ben had also been the victims of a killer. It came to me that I was in line for the same thing, but that concerned me far less than being able to accuse this murderer and have an eyewitness, of whom the murderer must be totally unaware, point him out. There'd be swift justice after that, I vowed.

I stepped into the elevator. "Hugo, why didn't you tell me about this before?"

"Didn't know anythin' about it, Miss Amy. It was only maybe a week ago my friend comes to me an' says he saw a man killed in the park. I asked him some questions and I figured it must have been your husband who got killed. But I didn't know where you were an' I didn't believe my friend at first anyway. He drinks some an' he was drunk when he told me about it. But I asked him again when he was dead sober, an' he said the same thing. I'm mighty glad you came back so I could tell you."

"Thank you," I said. He was so patiently looking for money as to be embarrassing, but I gave him nothing. Not then. If the man's story proved to be correct, I would see that Hugo got something for his trouble.

Back in Marion's dress shop, she and Judy were still trying to decide on the gown Marion would wear. Judy held up another primrose gown.

"What do you think?" she asked. "I'd say it was about right."

"It's lovely," I said. "Marion, may we postpone this for just a little while? I need to talk to Judy."

"Of course. I'll be here," Marion said. "Don't be in any hurry."

"Amy, what's the matter?" Judy asked as I hurried her through the lobby toward the elevator.

"I'll tell you as soon as we're in our suite. It's shocking, I can guarantee that much."

In the elevator Hugo gave me a knowing look, but he didn't speak. I closed the door to our suite and sat down heavily in one of the stuffed chairs. Judy remained standing, looking down at me, waiting for me to explain this sudden mystery.

"Judy, I have just learned from an eyewitness that Alex was murdered."

"What?" Judy collapsed into her chair. "Amy, you're not making this up?"

"In all the world I'd never make up a story like that."

"I'm sorry. I shouldn't have said that. I know you wouldn't. Tell me what happened."

"This witness was in the park. The murderer never saw him, never knew he was there. He says the murderer had set up some kind of a rope or wire that tripped Alex's horse so that Alex was thrown. As he lay on the ground—unconscious, I hope—this murderer struck him with some sort of weapon. It resulted in a wound that looked like it could have come from Alex's being thrown."

Judy clasped her hands so hard the knuckles turned white. "Who? Did he say who it was?"

"I don't know yet, except that it was a man. He kept calling the killer a 'gent.' I think he could have told me, but he was looking for money. A great deal of money, I expect. He is waiting to hear from me with instructions on how to reach the farm. He will come there and point out the man he saw."

"But, Amy, why do you think it was someone on the farm?"

"Because it's quite clear to me that Alex's brothers were also murdered, and by the same person. I always felt that Alex thought so too. The motive is clear enough. Someone wants the farm. I'm not accusing anyone on the farm, mind you. But someone killed Alex and I'm going to prove it."

"How awful," Judy said. "Have you any idea . . . ?"

"None. When the truth comes out, it won't be an idea. However, I'm not going to send for this man until after the ball. I don't want to disrupt that, and if I go into the situation now, there won't even be a ball. It can wait. So can I, as long as I know there is some proof of the man's identity in existence."

"There's only Len and Gordon."

"There could be someone else. Perhaps I'm all wrong in the motive too. I'm thinking of Carl Terrell."

"He's a strange one," Judy admitted. "And there's also Jess Foster."

"Why Jess?" I asked quickly.

"The family always suspected him of taking out the loss of his horse on the whole family, beginning with Merv. But, no, that can't be. Merv died before Jess lost that horse. Still, you never can tell."

"Oh, Judy, I almost wish we hadn't come here. Everything was beginning to settle down, but then, Alex was murdered and we cannot let that just go by."

"Do you think we can act normally, knowing this? While the dancing and music and everything goes on? I don't know if I trust myself."

"You'll have to. The ball must be gotten over with first. I so looked forward to it, but it's spoiled for me now. I don't know what to think, except that Alex's death is not going to be unavenged."

"I don't know what to say," Judith began lamely. "You're talking about my people. The only ones I have in the world. You're saying one of them is not only a murderer . . . but . . . but . . . we are all related. We're a family . . . and Alex was . . . I regarded him as if he were my brother. How could any of us have killed him? And that's what you're inferring, Amy."

"No, I am not," I contradicted her. "There is a motive there, true, but there may be a dozen others that we don't know about and that do not concern everyone. They're my family too now. Neither of us has anybody else, and I earnestly pray they are not guilty of this horrible crime."

"I would swear neither Len nor Gordon could have done such a thing."

"Nor I. Judy, we must not tell them about this. Nothing must be done until that witness arrives."

"I can't do that," Judy said. "I simply cannot, Amy. They have to know."

"You must not tell them, Judy. I beg you."

"You've been with us a few weeks, a few months. I've been with them all my life. I must tell them what you discovered. It isn't as if you went looking for this witness. You didn't even know he was alive. You discovered this by chance, and it may not even be true. But even so, I will tell Gordon. I have to."

"I wish I'd not told you anything about it," I said, discouraged by the whole thing and myself filled with doubt. I supposed if I was in her place I'd feel the same way, but I could only recall that Alex trusted none of them, not even Judy, who sat near me crying softly.

I said, "You know when Alex was killed. Was anyone absent for a time sufficient to reach New York and do this awful thing?"

She hesitated. "That's just it . . . I don't know. I wasn't there at the time. I returned right after you sent word about the tragedy. I'd been in Memphis visiting an old schoolmate."

"I hope you won't mind if I ask you the name and address of this friend."

Judy looked up quickly and once again that mask of hostility came over her face. I'd seen it before, especially at the moment she learned I was the heir and she would receive nothing.

"What for?" she asked tersely.

"I know you're telling me the truth, but it may become necessary that someone else knows you are not lying to protect your family."

"What a thing to say!"

"Put yourself in my place. My husband was killed and your family—it wasn't mine then—had good reason to kill him. You have already expressed your devotion to them, for which I blame you not at all. But others..."

"What others?" The hostility was still there.

"The police."

"Good God, you're not going to call them in?"

"Not now. That's why I don't want a word of this to be told to anyone until after the ball is over. Otherwise, there will be no ball. You surely understand that."

She nodded slowly. "I'm sorry I was so crusty. This has hit me too hard. I can't reconcile to it. It sounds like a weird dream."

"It's no dream to me, Judy. I loved Alex with all my heart. Someone murdered him and almost got away with it. I'll tell you this, I'm not now, and I never will be, in a forgiving mood. I want that murderer properly punished. Mostly because of what he did, but partly because of what he can still do. To me! I feel I'm in danger now."

She shook her head in exasperation. "I must tell them. I must!"

"You won't wait until after the dinner? You may spoil the whole thing."

"All those lovely gowns. I don't know what to do."

"The dinner and the ball are important to all of us. We can't allow that to not happen. The invitations are out. How do we explain the cancellation? Because we're looking for a murderer? Judy, be reasonable."

She nodded slowly. "I guess you're right. We can't do anything but have the ball, and telling Gordon, Len and— Oh, my God, what will this do to Veronica?"

"Keep it a secret. We can handle her better after the dinner. Promise, Judy?"

"I'll do my best. It's an awful secret."

"Murder is an awful thing. Perhaps this man who

claims he was an eyewitness is lying in an attempt to get money. The whole thing can be a lie. We have to wait."

"I know," Judy said in a small voice. "I know. You're right. You always are, Amy. I'll try to keep the secret."

6

Judy and I met Marion at the railroad station. She was dressed in a blue traveling suit that made Judy openly envious.

"If I only knew how to dress like that," she said.

"Knowing how to dress is her business," I reminded her. "But Marion's not trying to put on airs or make anyone jealous. She's not that kind of person."

I hugged Marion and so did Judy. A porter carried her bags to the carriage, which Judy drove. On the way to the farm we happily gossiped about fashions, Marion's more famous customers, and the ball. That's all we talked about at Greenlawn these days. The excitement of it even caused me to forget, momentarily at least, that my husband had been murdered and that there was a chance I was also in the same danger.

The farm fascinated Marion, who was, I discovered, a rather good rider. Everyone liked her, and Len was actually smitten by her. Len, who never seemed to care a fig for any woman and who was a confirmed and well-satisfied bachelor. So he had reminded me often enough.

There seemed to be no change in the family's attitude. Because of Marion's presence, Veronica maintained a degree of sobriety that proved what a gracious hostess she could be when she stayed away from drink.

With Marion's expert help, we soon had the decorations up in the dining room and we turned the drawing room into a huge would-be ballroom. The six-piece orchestra would play from a slightly raised dais banked with greenery and flowers.

Everything was in order the day of the ball. We dined lightly that midday and talked about the ball. In the afternoon, Marion, Judy, and I went for a brief ride before turning to the more important tasks of preparing ourselves.

When we returned to the stables, one of the hostlers took charge of our horses. Len was nowhere about. We returned to the house, and while Judy and Marion went to their rooms, I sought out Len. He admitted me to his suite of rooms and preened before a full-length mirror in his newly purchased formal wear.

He turned about, to smile somewhat foolishly. "I don't look much like the gentry, but I reckon I'll do."

"You look absolutely grand," I said. "I came to ask if you will be Marion's escort."

"Now why do you think I went and spent good money on this outfit?" he asked, as he still stood before the mirror admiring himself. "I do declare, Amy, you've changed this house all around. Happens I like it. I could get to like Marion too. I'm not the best dancer in the world, but I'll try my best not to destroy her shoes with my big feet, to say nothing of her toes."

"Good," I approved. "I never thought you'd leave the stables long enough to come to the ball."

"Likely wouldn't have if you'd not brought Miss Marion here."

"Will Carl see to the stables while the dancing is going on? Or should we have invited him?"

"Carl? He'd make a fool of himself, and us too.

Drinks too much and gets real cranky. The horses will be fine. Stablehands will see to that. Carl went off to race at Lexington. Good thing too, he needs some experience before he races Valiant at Cumberland. He'll be back tonight."

I went to join Judy and Marion in Judy's suite of rooms. Veronica was there too, and she and Marion got along splendidly. We tried on our gowns. Marion made a few changes, being so adept with needle and thread.

Marion's gown was almost the same color as mine and so was the styling, but the resemblance was not so great that it would be the subject of comment.

By midafternoon the first of the guests began to arrive, especially those who had driven great distances. It gratified all of us that of the more than a hundred invitations, only a few wrote to tell us illness or some previous engagement prevented them from coming. It was, I felt sure, going to be the grandest social affair in the county for some time to come.

The theme, of course, concerned horses and racing. Decorations consisted of blue and silver ribbons of large size, winner's horseshoe floral arrangements, servants dressed in racing colors, and dessert cakes in the form of racetracks.

It was all in excellent taste and motivated to inspire our guests to merriment and gaiety.

We all stood in the receiving line. Veronica looked lovely. She could seem to age considerably during her drinking bouts, but once sober, there were no telltale signs of what she had endured.

Dinner was lavish, at my request, and beautifully served. There were sufficient courses to keep everyone at the table for a long time, and the chattering that went on became a pleasant buzz of sound, pleasing me, for it was proof that everyone was thoroughly enjoying themselves.

They all liked Marion, the women especially, for they took advantage of every opportunity to question her about fashions. But one thing dampened the festivities as far as I was concerned. I had sent Jess Foster an invitation for himself and his mother to attend. He'd not replied and I'd not informed anyone of my inviting him, for I decided he was not going to come.

But not long after dinner, when the orchestra began to play the latest tunes for dancing, Jess suddenly appeared in the ballroom, somewhat desperately trying to locate me.

Gordon, who was near my side, uttered a mild expletive. "Who asked him?"

"I did," I said. "It's no more than right. He's one of our closest neighbors, and as I understand it, we've not been too neighborly with him."

"I wouldn't have invited him," Gordon grumbled. "But you certainly had the right to. I'll be as civil as I can, even though I don't like the man. Nor trust him."

Veronica was very gracious, going quickly to greet Jess like an old friend, but Judy outdid her by actually rushing to him when she suddenly discovered he was present. She clung to his arm and guided him to where Marion and I waited. I introduced him to Marion and I saw her glance at me with an amused expression, for she'd quickly noted the warm look in Jess's eyes when he took my hand.

I said, "As hostess, Judy, I insist on the first dance with Mr. Foster."

"So long as the second one is mine," Judy said gaily.

Jess and I danced to a slow waltz, which suited me fine. It gave us a chance to talk.

"My mother wouldn't come, of course," he said. "But I think she's been hearing things about you and she seems to be softening a bit. It's a fine party. I don't think you missed many people in the whole county."

"We tried not to," I said. "Jess, I want to talk to you later. Something serious has come up . . ." I caught myself. "But we won't spoil the party by such serious talk. This is a time to enjoy ourselves. Don't hold Judy too close or you'll make me jealous."

He smiled. "I like Judy, but only as a friend. A found-again friend, because I doubt she liked me very much until now. I noted Gordon glaring my way more than once. And, to my everlasting surprise, if that's not Leonard dancing with your friend."

"Or trying to," I said. "He's an admitted poor dancer, yet he tries and I'm grateful for that. I think he's smitten with Marion."

"Will you mind if I dance with Judy?" he asked. "I promise not to hold her that close. After all, she is an old friend, even if that friendship dwindled to nothing after the last Cumberland."

"Of course I don't mind. Judy's changed quite a bit. So have the others. Oh, my," I added as I glanced around, "Evelyn is here."

"Evelyn?" he asked in a puzzled voice.

"Evelyn Allison, Ben's fiancée. I must go to her."

"Of course," Jess agreed. "I won't be lonely," he added with a grin.

Judy, seeing us off the dance floor, was coming our way. "I don't doubt that, Jess. Will you dance with Evelyn later?"

"I'll look forward to it. I'll ask her as soon as I finish with Judy. But I won't stay late. Mama's angry that I came at all."

I left him to Judy and she was in his arms a moment later. I hurried toward the door to greet Evelyn, who hadn't been recognized by anyone yet. She looked sleek and marvelous in a dark-red gown.

"My dear," I said, and took both her hands, "it's wonderful of you to come."

"I felt I should," she said. "But I made up my mind so late that I was unable to find an escort. Seems all the young men were already coming to your party."

I led her to where Veronica and Gordon were the center of a group. Veronica immediately greeted Evelyn with a warm hug and even Gordon unbent enough to say he was happy to see her.

Evelyn said, "I want to talk to you for a moment, Amy. Some quiet place, if you don't mind."

I led her to the library and closed the door. "Is something wrong?" I asked.

"I don't know. There may be. On my way here, after I left my carriage, I met Ruth."

"Ruth?" I asked, momentarily confused by so many names I'd encountered tonight.

"The girl Merv was going to marry before he . . . died."

"Well, she's certainly welcome," I said. "I've not met her before. Will you point her out?"

"I don't think she came inside. She wasn't dressed for a party. And Ruth is a very strange person. She has always believed that since she and Merv were to be married, she should share in the good fortune of the farm. I believe Gordon sends her a little money from time to time, but it's not enough for her. She may be here to make trouble."

"I'll go out and try to find her," I said. "I don't want anything to spoil this affair. It's going along too well for that. But first I must tell you that Jess wants to dance with you."

"I saw him here. What on earth ever made him come?"

BRIDAL BLACK

"Me," I said. "I asked him. I like Jess even if the rest of the household doesn't. If anyone was seriously damaged by last year's race, I think it was Jess, and we have no reason to not like him."

"Well, good luck," Evelyn said. "He may not be bodily thrown out, but he may well be ostracized."

We returned to the ballroom and I waited with her until Jess finished his dance with Judy. She greeted Evelyn warmly and Jess danced off with her.

I said, "Ruth is somewhere outside. I'm going to see her if I can find her."

"Oh, damn," Judy said vehemently. "If she can break up this wonderful party..."

"She won't," I said. "But I think I'd best see her alone. Don't tell the others she's here."

"I don't envy you," Judy said with a grimace. "She can be a really nasty person."

I went outside. The night was warm, singularly so for this early in the season. The carriage drivers were all gathered at the rear of the house, where they were enjoying their own festivities. I saw Ruth seated on one of the concrete benches close by a formal garden, not yet in full bloom. She was a woeful sight, in a black skirt, a long dark-brown sweater, and a hat fashionable three or four years ago.

"Hello, Ruth," I said. "I'm Amy. Won't you please come inside?"

"Dressed like this?" she asked angrily. "Who told you I was here? Yes ... Evelyn, that tattletale. Well, I'm glad you came out. Thought you would. I got things to talk about."

I sat down beside her. "I'm a good listener, Ruth. I'm sorry you feel this angry with us, but I assure you I bear you no animosity."

"You came into this whole estate, didn't you? Just because you married Alex and didn't tell anybody about it."

"What difference did it make if I told anyone or not?" I asked.

"Makes the difference between him dying in New York or being killed here."

"What do you mean by that?"

"Isn't it plain enough? If they murdered two of the brothers, there's little reason they wouldn't murder the third."

"You speak of murder," I said. "What makes you believe it was murder?"

"They were after the estate. The lot of them. Well, what I want is simple enough. If I'd had a chance to marry Merv I'd be part of this and have all the money and clothes that you got. I never owned a dress like yours and it's my favorite color. I got jealous as soon as you stepped out of the house. I want part of this too. It's only fair I should get it."

"What precisely do you want?" I asked, horrified at her angry, direct approach and her accusations of murder.

"My share. That's all. Just my share."

"Ruth, that's not possible. You know it. But if Gordon isn't sending you enough, perhaps something can be done about that. However, I don't believe this family owes you anything, if the truth be told."

She jumped to her feet. "You're like the others. You have no heart, no sympathy. I wish you were dead!"

She turned and ran away in the direction of the stables. There was nothing I could do. She wouldn't stop if I called to her, and I was quite content that she didn't wish to enter the house and join the festivities, for I guessed she would have made an issue of her enviousness in front of everyone. I did shudder slightly at her wishing me dead. I'd never before had the experience of listening to anything like that.

Judy came to me the moment I entered the house, a question on her lips. "She's an angry, frustrated girl," I said. "I couldn't do anything with her; I wonder why she came here."

"I can tell you that. To let herself get angrier at us because we're giving this ball; it makes her hatred mount when we spend all this money that she thinks she is entitled to. Poor Merv would have led an awful life with her."

"I'm so sorry for her. I intend to talk to Gordon about trying to pacify her somewhat."

"Money will do that. Only money, and there isn't enough of it in the world to satisfy her. I wouldn't give her a cent, but then I'm more hardhearted than you. Jess is in love with you. Did you know that?"

"Jess? Why, Judy, what a thing to say! Good heavens, I barely know the man."

"It's too soon after Alex's death, but someday he's going to come courting. I can tell by the way he talks about you and the way he looked whenever you came into view."

"Are you in love with him, Judy?" I asked. "Tell me the truth."

"I . . . don't know. I thought I was and I was so happy to see him, but now I'm not sure. I won't stand in your way, Amy."

"Now, Judy," I remonstrated with her, "you cannot stand in the way of something that does not exist."

"It will. Sooner or later it will. Here he comes, and he's not looking at me, worse luck."

Jess promptly claimed me for the next dance. I recalled what Judy had said and I realized that I felt so comfortable and secure in Jess's arms. He reminded me of Alex because of his warmth and his obvious sincerity.

As we danced, I looked about the crowded room. "I don't see Marion. Weren't you dancing with her?"

"Three times," he said. "She's an amazing woman. I think she knows more of what goes on in the world than I do."

"Where is she?" I asked.

"She went out for some air. I would have gone with her, but she just wanted to take a little walk alone. She complained that it was warm in here."

"It surely is," I agreed. "Are you enjoying yourself?"

"You have no idea. But this is my last dance. I don't like leaving my mother alone too long. It's not that she demands this of me, but she does have a bad heart and when I'm away I worry about her."

"I'm sorry you have to leave so soon, Jess. I do hope you will come again. It's time this animosity is over and done with. At least Judy is now on your side."

"I'm glad of that. She's a nice girl—when she wants to be. I hope that you will come to call on me too."

"I'll ride over tomorrow," I said. "Something's happening at the farm that scares me half to death. I want to talk to you about it."

"Of course. I'll be glad to help in any way I can."

He said good night a few moments after we finished the dance. He approached Veronica and Gordon, and Gordon was more tolerant of him. I was sure this long period of enmity was going to end. I hoped so.

Len came by, and his meeting with Jess was far warmer. He shook hands with him, pounded him on the back, and they talked for a few moments. Then Len reached my side as Jess departed.

"At the risk of injury, would you dance with me, Amy?"

"Why, Len, you know I've been looking forward to it all evening."

"Yes, perhaps, but you didn't say whether it was to being injured or dancing with me."

He was not as clumsy as I thought he might be, and we danced a gavotte without his kicking me in the shins, which was akin to a miracle, for the gavotte was certainly a fast and rather intricate dance.

"I've missed Marion," he said as we walked off the dance floor. "Now there's a woman for me. Seems likable as all get-out. Besides she never once complained about my clumsiness."

"You don't give yourself credit, Len. You're a fine dancer. Jess told me Marion went out to get some air."

"Alone?" he asked. "That shouldn't be. Excuse me. I'm going to find her."

I danced with Gordon, who seemed to have something on his mind that threatened to burst from him if he didn't express himself.

"You're so quiet," I said. "Is anything wrong, Gordon?"

"Judy told me what happened in New York."

"Oh!" All the joy went out of me. "I asked her not to say anything until the party was over. She shouldn't have really, because this is one night I didn't want spoiled."

"She was worried about Ruth being around the place, and when I cornered her about why she was worried, she told me about that man who says he saw Alex being killed."

"Gordon, we'll talk about it tomorrow. There is much to talk over. I shall send for this man soon, but not until we have argued it all out here. The man may be mistaken, he may not have seen anything and is just looking for money. I don't know, but I want to be sure he has something to contribute before I send for him, which is why we should talk first."

"There's nothing to talk about. The whole thing is silly, Amy. Downright preposterous."

"Perhaps. We shall see. Now, no more of this tonight. The ball has still a long way to go. Does Len know?"

"I haven't dared tell him. He'll cut up some when he hears about it, and he's not exactly quiet when he gets angry."

Len came back, not having found Marion.

"Don't worry," I told him. "She told Jess she wanted to be alone for a while. She'll be all right."

I danced half a dozen dances with men who had signed my dance card, and despite all the sudden trouble, it was a good evening. Before everyone left there was a buffet to sustain our guests on their long journeys home.

This was set up in the dining room so the ballroom was fairly well cleared when I saw Carl rush into the house. He looked about, saw me. His face was a pasty gray color. He saw Len and went to him as fast as he could maneuver his way. Len listened to him a moment, grasped his wrist, and pulled him out of one of the french windows leading onto the estate. I heard them running in the direction of the stables, and my heart stopped beating for a moment. Something was wrong, definitely wrong, and it concerned Marion, who apparently had not yet returned from her walk.

I found Gordon. "Carl just came in looking like he'd seen a ghost. He and Len went off to the stables. I'm afraid something is wrong."

Gordon turned and hurried away. I followed him, but he didn't wait for me and I was compelled to hike up my gown and try to run after him. By the time I reached the stables, Gordon was turning back. He stopped me by putting his arms around me.

"I wouldn't go down there," he said. "She's dead. Your friend is dead. It looks like she went into the stall of that black stallion and . . . the horse killed her."

I pressed my head against his chest and wept. I blamed myself. I should never have asked her to this house. It was a place of murder and death. There was something evil here. The girls who would have been brides all wore black instead of a wedding gown. And now poor Marion, who never knew what it was about, was dead. I never believed for a moment but that she had been murdered, even before I learned all the circumstances.

Gordon said, "You've got to bear up to this. All our guests haven't gone yet and it's best they know nothing of it until later. Brace up. We'll say our goodbyes as quickly as we can. Don't tell Veronica about it yet. She's bound to go to pieces."

I couldn't even answer him. He gave a few details of what he knew about the tragedy as we walked back to the house.

"Carl just came back. He was away for the last couple of days. He heard that stallion making a fuss and went to see what was wrong. He found her. Apparently she heard the stallion making a fuss too, and she must have gone into the stall to try and quiet the animal without knowing that horse was dangerous. All the stablehands are at the party for the help and the drivers, so nobody was near the stables."

We were both startled to hear a gunshot. For a moment my terror began to make me shiver.

"It's the stallion," Gordon said. "Len told me he was going to shoot the beast. That's all it was. No need to be scared."

"Gordon, I am afraid. You don't really think Marion was killed by accident?"

"Now what . . . ?"

"She was wearing a gown almost the exact color of mine. Someone killed her."

"For wearing a gown . . . ?"

"The murderer thought I was the person he killed. He made a mistake, and I don't think he'll make another. That's why I'm afraid."

7

We left the servants to clean up after the last carriage departed. Then Len and Carl brought Marion's body to the house and we placed it in the room I'd assigned her. I looked at her body only briefly, for she'd been so badly mauled as to make my stomach turn. Judy fainted into Gordon's arms.

We went downstairs and into the gaudily decorated ballroom still smelling of perfumes and perhaps a little sweat. There we sat down to consider the situation.

We were all present: Len, Veronica, Judy, Gordon, Carl, and I. They waited for me to take charge of the situation.

I said, "Carl, tell us what you discovered."

"Ain't much to tell. I came in from Lexington. I heard the party going on, but I was tired and I intended to go to bed. I heard the stallion kicking the stall to pieces and I went to quiet him down. I saw something on the floor of the stall that seemed to be making the horse nervous. Then I saw it was this woman. I didn't know who she was. Never saw her before, far as I know."

"She was my friend from New York," I said. "You were not here when she arrived. When you reached the stall, was the stall door unlatched?"

Carl frowned. "I don't know. Damn if I remember. I was too excited to notice."

"It couldn't have been," Gordon said quickly. "How could she have latched it after going inside?"

"If what I think Amy is thinking," Len said, "somebody else may have latched it so she couldn't get out once the horse started rampaging."

"I don't know what you mean," Carl said.

"Never mind," I said. "Try to remember if the stall door was latched."

"I . . . think it was. What I did, I did without thinking. It all happened so fast. . . ."

"Thank you," I said. "Did you see anyone around the stables?"

"Nobody. All the help was at the party for the drivers and coachmen. Nobody was around."

"Amy," Judy asked, "do you really think Marion was murdered? What reason on earth was there to kill her?"

Gordon answered for me. "Amy pointed out that Marion wore the same color gown as hers, and they're about the same build. She thinks someone mistook Marion for her and it was Amy who should have been killed."

"If that's true," Len said, "it had to be done by somebody who knew that stallion was a killer. And Marion would not just have entered that stall to quiet that particular horse because anybody who knows horseflesh—and she did—would not have even gone near that horse."

"Go on," I said. "Tell the rest of it, Len."

"She must have been thrown into the stall. And she must have been knocked out first. There was a bad laceration on the back of her head that didn't look to me like it was caused by the stallion."

"Now," I said, "we have four murders. What are we to do about it?"

"The man in New York—" Judy began.

"What man?" Len asked.

"You haven't been told," Gordon said. "When Judy and Amy were in New York, Amy was approached by some man who said he saw Alex being thrown from his horse by a trap, and then killed by a man this informant says he can recognize."

"Well, where is he? This man," Len demanded.

"I didn't send for him because of the ball," I explained. "That was my mistake. I shall send for him at once."

"Who," Len asked, "could have done this? I mean, Marion's murder. I don't think the boys were murdered, no matter what this witness says. But Marion—yes. And because there wasn't the vaguest possible reason for killing her, I agree that whoever did it mistook her for you, Amy."

"We've got to notify the authorities," Gordon said. "And arrange about sending the body back . . . or whatever is to be done with it. I know so little about Marion."

"She had no one," I said. "Nobody at all close. She loved it here. I ask that she be buried in the family plot."

"Of course, of course," Gordon said. "I'll see to her business in New York. Do whatever is necessary."

"Thank you," I said.

Veronica, who sat wordlessly and very erect in one of the tall chairs, suddenly arose. She left the drawing room, but when she passed through it a few seconds later, she was carrying, quite openly, a bottle of brandy. She said nothing but went slowly up the stairs. We heard her bedroom door slam shut.

I arose quickly. Gordon grasped my elbow. "It's no use, Amy. Let her go. It's even better that way. For her. Please sit down again and let's try to guess who could have done this awful thing."

I sat down, knowing he was right about Veronica. I said, "As far as I can recall, Gordon never left the party. Nor did Judy or Veronica. Len, you left the dance."

"Looking for Marion. I never thought of checking the stables."

"Carl wasn't here," I said.

"I told you, I just got back..."

"Yes, I know, Carl. Whatever happened to Evelyn? She didn't even say good night."

"I hadn't seen her after ten o'clock," Gordon said.

"And there was Ruth," I reminded them. "The last words she said to me as she hurried away was to the effect that she wished I was dead."

"She'll have to explain that," Gordon assured me.

"And Jess..." Judy declared softly. "He went off early."

"Judy, what a thing to say," Gordon remonstrated. "Why would Jess...?"

"Why would anybody?" Judy demanded. "Why anything? Why did this have to happen? It's all a bunch of whys and they don't make any sense. A perfectly innocent woman was probably murdered here because she was mistaken for Amy. Don't ask why. We know why! Ask who!"

"That's what we've been doing. With no answers," I said. "I suggest we go to bed. It's been a long, long day and it ended in horror. Perhaps we're not in shape to analyze this very well now. It can wait until morning and then we'll leave it to the authorities. I can't take any more. Please excuse me." I walked toward the door and stopped. Everyone looked at me with open curiosity as to what I was going to say next.

"Carl," I said, "please wait a few moments. I'm going into the library and write out a telegram. It's to a person I know, who knows the man who saw Alex murdered. I understand it is now possible to arrange with the telegraph company to relay money to someone in the big cities. I shall give you a hundred dollars to be used for that purpose. To pay the man to come here. Perhaps then we can settle this awful thing. That's all. Be sure to wait, Carl, and send the telegram as soon as you can."

"And as soon as you attend to that chore," Gordon added, "tell the sheriff what happened and get Mr. Garrett here."

"Garrett is the undertaker," Judy explained for my benefit.

We were all exhausted, but until Marion's body was removed, none of us could sleep. And when we did go to bed, it was only to be awakened by the arrival of the sheriff, who had been elsewhere in the county on business and came out as soon as he returned and heard the news.

The sheriff, a man named Lambert, was heavyset, an intelligent man, well-versed in law and order. He questioned me first, as head of the household, and I told him all I could, omitting any information about the man in New York whom I had sent for.

"My friend was unknown here," I explained. "She'd never been in Virginia in her life. There could be no reason for striking her down and throwing her into the stall with a half-mad horse. In my opinion she was mistaken for me."

"And why you? " Lambert asked in his quiet way, suggestive of great strength behind it and determination he'd never satisfy until it was all settled.

"My husband and his two brothers all met violent deaths, each being thrown from a horse. Each would have come into the ownership of this farm, but the legacy was passed on until it reached me. I married Alex Paige and I came here to claim his estate."

"You're inferring that somebody else wants the estate and killed the three brothers to get it? And then concentrated on you?"

"It may sound absurd, but that's what I think. It's what we all think."

"It's not as absurd as it sounds, Mrs. Paige. I've wondered about the deaths of Ben and Merv, and when I heard Alex was also killed, I did ask a few questions, but I didn't get anywhere. Do you suspect anyone?"

"No," I said. "I cannot conceive of anyone in this household being guilty of such a crime, or series of crimes."

"Who," he asked, "was not present at the ball at the time this happened?"

"I know Veronica was here. I'm sure Gordon never left the ballroom. Len did, but only for a short while. Judith left at no time."

"And Carl, the jockey?"

"He discovered the body when he heard the horse carrying on. Carl had just arrived from Lexington, where he'd been in a race. That's what he told us."

"It's the truth," Len said.

"I'll talk to him," Lambert said.

"He's at the stables," Len told him. "If he balks at answering questions, tell him I'll fire him if he doesn't tell all he knows."

"Thanks." Mr. Lambert rose, closing the notebook into which he'd been jotting down the facts as we had told them. He left to look for Carl.

Gordon glanced at me with a slightly twisted smile. "No one mentioned Jess Foster," he said.

"I rather thinks he knows all about Jess," Judy said. "It was well-known how angry he was when his horse was beaten by Valiant."

"Lambert's no fool," Len said. "Don't underestimate that man. And when he gets his teeth into something, he never lets go. We'll hear more from him."

"Tell me, Amy," Gordon asked, "why you didn't mention that man from New York who claims he can identify whoever killed Alex?"

"Because this man is an unsavory type. He hates the police and is afraid of anyone with a badge of authority. I'm afraid if he came down here and discovered he had to talk to a sheriff, he'd go back to New York without saying a word."

"Lambert's going to be mighty put-out you kept this from him," Len said.

"I can't help that," I said. "This is no time to take chances. We have to rely on this man, until we discover if he knows anything or not. I think Sheriff Lambert will understand."

"We can hope," Gordon said. "When is he due?"

"Carl sent the telegram this morning very early, I presume," I said. "I asked the man to come directly here. To hire a buggy, ask directions, and drive it to the farm. I expect he will arrive tomorrow. He won't linger because he's a greedy little man and wants money."

"Then we can do nothing but wait?" Judy asked.

"We have much to do," I reminded them. "There's Marion."

"They'll bring her back first thing in the morning," Gordon said. "A man is coming out today to dig the grave. Next week I'll go to New York and take care of her belongings and the store."

I shed a few tears as he spoke. There'd scarcely been time to really weep for this wonderful woman who had apparently given up her life for me. Unknowingly perhaps, but that made no difference.

After our noonday meal I put on my riding habit and went down to take Gracie out. Len had her saddled, and while we waited, he expressed himself at the death of Marion.

"She was the first woman who ever made me think twice about getting married. I'd have asked her, when I got the nerve. Never met any woman I liked more. I feel like I lost part of my life, even if I only knew her such a short time."

"She'd have been delighted to hear you say that, Len. I appreciate it also. I'm going to ride over to Jess's and talk to him. Perhaps he knows nothing, but it's worth the visit."

"I can tell you he knows about what happened last night. Sheriff Lambert left here to pay Jess a visit."

"Do you think he suspects him?"

"Well, you were not here when Jess was hollering his head off about being cheated by us. He said a few things then that won't do him any good now."

"Len, what really happened with Jess's horse just before the Cumberland?"

"I don't know. Carl was riding the horse, and it sure looked like somebody hid a lot of bramble bushes behind a jump that Carl always took the horse over. Carl could have gotten his fool neck broken. He was lucky. He swears he has no idea of how it happened, or who hid the brush behind the jump."

"But someone did?"

"Well, it looks that way, but I've seen a good wind blow all sorts of brush around. Those bushes had been cut a couple of days before and left in the open. There was some wind about that time. It's possible they blew around and lodged at the jump. I'm not saying that's what happened, I'm saying its possible."

"Thank you, Len, for being so helpful. I appreciate it."

I rode quite slowly toward Jess's farm. I didn't

want to run into Sheriff Lambert. He might wonder why I want to see Jess so soon after Lambert had questioned all of us. During the ride I tried to guess who might have killed Marion. I was sure that she'd been mistaken for me. So confident of that I never gave any thought to any other possible motive.

As far as I knew, nobody had left the ball except Len, Jess, and Evelyn. I understood that Sheriff Lambert was going to question her and Ruth later in the day, for we'd told him about their presence and Ruth's threat to me.

It was impossible for me to think that Judy had anything to do with the murder of the three brothers. As for their mother, Veronica was instantly ruled out. Gordon and Len would have profited if I'd not unexpectedly appeared on the scene. Whoever killed Alex did so in New York so he'd not have a chance to marry me, not knowing, of course, that we were already secretly married. I did give considerable thought to Carl, but he appeared to be sufficiently open and honest in his statements.

I saw Jess waiting for me as I rode up. One look at him and nothing in the world would have made me believe he could be capable of any crime.

He helped me down and for a moment held my hand without saying anything. Then we walked toward the house. "Sheriff Lambert was here," he said. "I'm stunned by the news he brought. It seems he thinks Marion was mistaken for you."

"That's what I told him and I believe it," I said.

"Yes, I can't see any reason for killing Marion. She'd only been here a very short time. Will you come in? Mother wants to apologize for the way she acted when you came here the first time."

I was promptly kissed on the cheek by his mother when we entered the remarkably well-furnished house. Though the mansion I'd inherited was a lovely place, this was more like a cozy home. I could feel its warmth surround me as I sat down in a padded rocker.

I went into more detail about some of the facts Sheriff Lambert had not elaborated on. From Mrs. Foster I received more information than I expected.

"Now mind you," she said, "I'm not a gossip, but I've known this for a long time. I never even told Jess because, when it happened, it didn't seem to be any of my business. Merv and Ruth were not in love. She played up to him because she knew he had money and she's a greedy girl. She was in a family way when Merv agreed to marry her. Right after he was killed, she went off somewhere and . . . whatever she had done, there was no baby. I know this because she came to me asking for money. I gave her some because I felt sorry for her, but later I learned what kind of a girl she was. And I think, if my opinion is worth anything, that she came to the ball you gave for a purpose. She never did anything without a reason."

"Perhaps it was only to ask me for more money," I said. "Gordon has been sending her some and she complained to me it wasn't enough."

"I hope that's why she came, but she is a vicious person. I told that to Sheriff Lambert. I hope I did not interfere with anything you told him."

"I'm sure you didn't, Mrs. Foster. I'd like it if you showed me about your farm, Jess. I came here ignorant of anything to do with a farm or horses, but I've learned much and I'd like to know more."

"I'll have a snack ready when you get back," his mother said. "We're quite proud of our farm, Amy. It's not like yours, but we think it will be someday."

"If I can help it along the way," I said, "you know you can call on me."

"All we want to do is win the Cumberland next

month," she said. "We need nothing more than that."

"Then, even at my own expense, I hope you do."

"That's a real nice thing to say, Amy. I get sorrier all the time for treating you the way I did."

Jess escorted me down to the stable, where I brought him to a halt by taking his arm. "I'm in need of your advice," I said. "I can't go to anyone on my farm for reasons that will be obvious to you when I tell you what has happened. Or is happening."

He led me to two chairs tilted back against the wall of a barn. We sat down in the warm sunlight and I told him about the mysterious horse running our track in the middle of the night.

"Are you sure?" he asked in amazement. "You could have been dreaming."

"It was no dream. It happened more than once. The last time I found Carl awake and he said it was a rampaging horse. The one that killed my friend last night."

"Carl is a liar. I don't believe that's possible—to sound like a running horse. He's a great jockey, though, and surely knows horses. I was sorry I had to fire him after he took that jump and my entry in the Cumberland was injured."

"Tell me, why is my family about to unveil a statue to the horse that won the last Cumberland? He is called Valiant."

"It's somewhat of a trick," Jess said. "It's been done before and usually works. The Cumberland Stakes is open to horses three years old and older. They donate the statue of a horse that won the Cumberland, and reenter that horse. The statue reminds folks what a great animal he is. They expect he'll win and they bet, quite heavily. The statue impresses them and reminds them that was the horse that won last time."

"But what does the family gain?" I asked. "Does all that betting on Valiant bring them any kind of reward?"

"The only thing a winning horse can claim is the purse. It's not exactly a big one this year."

"Then why go to all this trouble?"

"It could be vanity. Gordon is a vain man. Len is a man who is anything but vain, except where a horse is concerned. Valiant is his pet. He'd like a statue of him placed at the racetrack."

"I still don't see why they wish to exercise a horse by night?"

"Amy, if they have a horse hidden, being trained when no one is about, even by night, then they may believe they have a stronger horse that can be quietly entered. And a horse they think will beat everything that races that day. It's not a fair way to do things, but the track rules are somewhat lax. They will be made stronger soon, I'm sure, but right now that could be done."

"Then your horse can be beaten," I said. "By an animal you don't even know exists."

"That's the way it's done sometimes."

"In this instance it will not be done," I said firmly.

"How can you arrange that?"

"If there is a horse hidden on my farm, that horse belongs to me. I can refuse to allow the entry of that animal in any race, and I will, Jess. This time you're going to have a chance. If Valiant beats your horse, so be it, but no one is going to take a victory away from you by trickery."

"I'd know better what to say if I had a chance to see this animal."

I grew excited enough to rest my hand on his arm as I spoke. "I share that curiosity with you and I'll do something about it. If you agree, let's meet at about one o'clock in the morning day after tomorrow. We'll wait and watch. If nothing happens, we'll search every stall. Of course, we have a great many horses, and if there is a strange one, I'd never know it. Would you know?"

"Sometimes the build of a horse gives away the fact that he's a fine race animal. I can at least try."

"Then shall we meet at one o'clock? Not tonight, but tomorrow night. Not by the stables, but near the gate to the track. In the darkness we'd never be seen."

"I'll be there," he said. "This is quite a conspiracy we're cooking up, but it is necessary. You say you heard the horse running by night. How does it happen none of the stablehands heard it?"

"Most of them don't live on the farm," I explained. "Those that do, have their families with them and they occupy cabins some distance from the track. I'm sure they'd not be apt to hear any horse running by night."

"Then maybe we can settle this. Did you ever mention it to anyone else?"

"I asked Carl about it, but as I said, he tried to tell me it was that wild horse making the racket."

"I wouldn't be apt to believe anything Carl said. Amy, I know it's very soon after Alex, but . . . would you resent my coming to call? As a friend. I like you very much."

I knew what he was trying to tell me and I appreciated the way he did it. I liked him too. I didn't know if it could ever blossom into love, but I realized it might, after a suitable time had passed. For now, it was much too soon and not to be considered. The memory of Alex was too fresh. Yet there'd be no harm in seeing Jess.

I said, "Of course, Jess. I'd be very happy to see

you. Shall I tell you why? You are just like Alex. Everything you do reminds me of him. I believe you'll be a great comfort to me."

"I'm glad," he said. "Very happy. We could go riding together, for one thing."

"I'd enjoy that too. But first we must solve this mystery of a horse that can run in the dark and vanish into the night. Besides finding out who may possibly wish me dead."

"I'll do whatever I can to protect you, Amy. That, too, will be my privilege."

We walked back to the house, where I enjoyed the tea and some of the tastiest cookies I'd ever eaten, and a pleasant conversation with Jess's mother. It was almost dusk by the time we finished chatting. I didn't want to be riding in the dark, so I excused myself and with the help of Jess's boot up, I managed to make the saddle quite gracefully, somewhat to my own surprise.

I rode away feeling better than I had since Marion had been killed. And Jess did remind me of Alex so much. I wanted him to call on me. I gave absolutely no thought to the fact that there were those who believed he might have killed Marion.

8

There was a slight chill in the air as I rode back. It was more invigorating than unpleasant. I was quite proud of myself for the way I rode now, for I'd mastered most of the fundamentals in what I thought was a respectably brief period. Of course, Len had provided me with the gentlest of horses and I'd become quite attached to Gracie.

For so much of my time at Greenlawn, my mind had been in a state of turmoil. So many things had happened and I had so much to adjust to. And to have it develop into the murder of Marion, augmented by the knowledge it was I who should have been killed rather than she, filled me with strong apprehension. So, suddenly, my mind seemed to be at rest, even in the midst of the latest problem of the murder. Perhaps due to the quiet talk I'd had with Jess's mother, combined with the knowledge that she no longer hated me. And with the attitude Jess betrayed in his quiet way.

So, as my horse trotted down the road between tall forest growths, I was utterly unprepared for what happened with a suddenness that made my head whirl. There was a single shot. I heard it plainly enough, even though at that very moment my horse suddenly collapsed, dropping to her front knees and propelling me over her head to land with a stunning force.

I couldn't get up. I knew I must, because danger was closing in all around me. But every muscle was paralyzed. I managed to turn on my side and, somewhat dimly, realized there were no flashes of pain, so it was unlikely I'd broken any bones.

I saw Gracie, lying on her side, legs twitching in what seemed to be a dying agony. Blood ran down, matting her lovely mane. Perhaps it was this sight that roused me, for I pushed myself into a sitting position. I recalled the gunshot, I knew that Gracie had been wounded, likely killed. I could not risk just lying here, waiting for my murderer to walk up and put a bullet through me.

No more than a few seconds had elapsed since I pitched over the horse's head, though it seemed much longer. I struggled to my feet, paused for a moment to look down at the horse, and the sight of all that blood sickened me and brought out an intense hatred for whoever had done this awful thing.

Then reason took possession of my dulled wits and I realized I had to move quickly into some kind of shelter to avoid being a target. I tried to run straight for the protection of the forest, but it was more like a zigzag retreat, which was probably the reason why the second bullet only sang its deadly song a few feet from me. This spurred me into faster steps and I plunged into the forest. I kept going until I was out of breath and beginning to develop a severe headache as a result of the fall.

I collapsed. I couldn't go on. But a few moments later I heard someone moving about, and terror provided enough strength for me to move slowly and carefully deeper into the forest. When I stopped again, I heard the steps of the murderer once more. There seemed to be no getting away from him.

I thought about climbing a tree, but I wasn't even sure that I could. And should I be there, lodged on some limb, I'd be a doomed target. It was better to keep moving. To listen and apply stealth to stay away from whoever searched for me.

I realized I couldn't keep on much longer. It had been dusk riding down the road, and now, in the middle of a thick forest, it was rapidly turning to real darkness. I could barely see my way and I was in terror of stumbling against something that would create sufficient sound to give away my position.

With that in mind, I selected an old oak with a large trunk. I sat down and placed my back against it. Once I thought I heard the prowler, but after that, there was only the kind of strange silence that the midst of a forest can create.

At least I was resting. I could feel strength flowing back into my muscles and I trembled less. I had no inclination to move, for I was still badly shaken, so I remained where I was and with the passing minutes I felt surer that my would-be murderer had given up. I guessed that whoever he might be, there would be the need for establishing himself somewhere else so he could not be placed under suspicion. I decided I was now safe, for the time being. I had few doubts but that there would be another attempt at some time favorable to the man who'd just shot my horse and placed me in the midst of a forest at night.

It was totally dark now and I had lost all sense of direction. I knew that if I moved about at random, seeking the road, I might only go deeper into the forest and become completely lost. As if I wasn't right now.

I couldn't even see if I was backtracking. In the dark I had no signs to look for. I could easily be going around in a circle. I was frightened too. The attempt on my life had left me filled with apprehension, so that the idea of being lost became terrifying. In my mind these practically virginal forests seemed full of wild animals. Of what nature they might be I had no idea, but I brought bears and wolves to mind and it was not comforting.

I must have spent an hour or more just walking slowly, being hit in the face by low branches, tugged at by heavy brush. I knew my riding habit was torn in more than one place when I had to pull myself free of some restraining thorn.

I thought I heard a faint sound. It wasn't human and that made it all the more scary. It came again and I realized it was the whinny of a horse. It seemed to originate from my left. I didn't think it could be Gracie. The last I'd seen of her, she appeared to have been in the throes of death. Still, it was a sound I could use for direction, if it would only come again. It also meant that if this was a horse, I couldn't be very far from the road. I doubted any horse would venture into a thick forest by night. I also thought that where there was a horse, there'd likely be a rider. I moved very carefully.

I heard it again. I made my way in that direction, and several more now plainly whinnies gave me a signal I could readily follow. I came out onto the road at last and I felt as if I'd been released from a dark prison.

I couldn't see a horse. The darkness prevented that. I called out, and there was a movement directly ahead of me. I walked fast now, trying to pierce the night for a sign of whatever animal was making those sounds. Desperation made me forget the caution I'd used so far.

I saw the dark form then, and without fear, I hurried toward it to find that it was Gracie, after all. I was so surprised and happy that I began to cry. I laid my head against Gracie's quivering flank and let the tears come. But soon I was stroking her muzzle. I felt the stickiness of the blood that had come from the wound, but it couldn't have been a serious one. Just something that brought on a weakness or a quick unconsciousness.

I didn't have the heart to try to swing up into the saddle. Gracie might be seriously hurt and I didn't want to risk injuring her any more. So I held on to the bridle and we walked back to the farm. It was a two-mile journey, but I made it without faltering and Gracie held up as well.

I led her straight to the stables. Someone called my name. It was Gordon. I shouted to reveal my whereabouts. In a few moments they were all coming toward me—Gordon, Judy, Len, and Carl. Veronica was likely in no condition to even leave her rooms.

"Where in the world have you been?" Gordon asked.

Len and Carl held lanterns and they turned the light on me and the horse. Len swore softly.

"What happened to the horse?" he demanded, as if he thought I was to blame.

"She was shot," I explained. "Someone, a couple of miles back on the road, shot the horse and I was thrown. I thought Gracie was dead. I ran away. I couldn't help the animal then. Someone fired another shot at me and missed. I ran into the forest and stayed there until dark. Whoever it was, came searching for me. I could hear him moving about. When it got very dark and there were no more sounds, I tried to find my way out of the forest, but I suppose I was just walking in a circle. Then Gracie whinnied and I was able to find her. Is she badly hurt, Len?"

Len and Carl were bringing their lanterns closer. Len said, "She's lost a lot of blood, looks like."

"Skinned her knees some too," Carl reported. He

ran his hands up and down her legs. "Nothing busted."

Len walked over to face me. "You know what that skunk did. He creased Gracie. Fired a shot that got her through the neck. It never kills a horse, but it knocks them out and they fall like they're dead. Did you get a look at him?"

"Not even a glimpse," I said sadly. "I wish I had."

"I suppose," Gordon said, "you're going to ask which of us could have done such a thing. I, for one—"

"I am not going to ask," I said. "Whoever did this is clever enough to have made it all but impossible to identify him. Or among you there may be more than one who cannot rightfully account for himself. No, I shall not ask questions, but during my lonely walk back I made up my mind what I intend to do about this. When I have completed what I plan, I shall tell all of you what my idea is. For now I want to take a bath, eat something—not much—and go to bed."

Judy put an arm around my waist and we walked slowly into the house and directly upstairs. While I bathed, Judy had a tray prepared for me and she sat at the small table in my parlor while I ate.

"Whether you ask or not, I'm going to try and tell you who was around and who wasn't. Gordon grew worried over your long absence and saddled a horse to go searching. He came back right after dark because he said it was not possible to search anymore until morning. I stayed with Veronica. She was in a bad way. Sometimes too much brandy makes her weep and carry on so. I don't know where Leonard was. He never came near the house, not even for supper. Carl, of course, does not come for meals, so I didn't see him either. That's how it was, Amy. The day started with a funeral and almost ended in another."

"It's going to stop," I vowed. "Tomorrow I want the use of a buggy. I'm going to ride into town."

"I'll go with you...."

"I must do this alone, Judy. Not that I don't wish you could come along. Let me say this now. I know you haven't any part in whatever is happening here. I feel that you're the only person I can really trust."

"Thank you," Judy said quietly. "I'll go now so you can get some sleep. I'll take the tray."

I slept well that night. It must have been due to exhaustion and nothing else, for when I lay down, my head was spinning with wild thoughts and I began to develop some measure of fear that sleep so kindly put an end to.

In the morning I found myself stiff and I saw the black-and-blue marks I'd developed from being thrown. I dressed, went down to breakfast, to find I was alone. Lena served me and clucked her tongue over my story of being pitched from the horse. I didn't elaborate, but I had to explain the bruises on my arms and a definite bump on my temple.

Judy had left word about the buggy, for when I was ready to leave, it waited for me just below the veranda steps. I got aboard and drove, with some trepidation, to the town. Anywhere along that route I could have been ambushed again, and I knew it.

It was with a strong sense of relief that I entered Mr. Taber's office late in the morning. I'd never been there before and I identified myself. I was immediately ushered into the lawyer's private office.

He came from behind his desk to take my hand in greeting. "Welcome, Mrs. Paige. I'm very happy to see you." He noted the bruised arm. "What happened?"

"I wasn't beaten up," I said. "But I was shot at, my

horse was . . . Len called it something . . . creased, I think he said. Anyway the horse was stunned by the bullet and I sailed over her head. Then someone shot at me again."

"My dear," he said, "what's going on to cause this?"

"Two days ago, during the ball we gave, a good friend of mine was killed and I think whoever killed her believed it was me. Someone is bent on murdering me, Mr. Taber. I want to put a stop to it."

"I should think so. I heard about that poor woman's death. Tell me what you've decided. I can see there's something."

I sat down and he resumed his chair behind the desk. "In my opinion someone wants the farm enough to resort to murder. I believe Alex and his brothers were killed to avoid any part of the farm passing on to their heirs, which they would have had if they lived long enough to marry. You will recall that before the will was read they all believed Alex and I never had the opportunity to marry."

"Yes, I have given that some thought myself, but it seemed so impossible. Do you suspect anyone?"

"I suspect them all, and that's why I wish to have you prepare a will. I want it very definitely stated that I have only one heir, Jess Foster. Even if it might be very hard to make it legal, they'll at least know there'd be a long court fight involved if I should die."

Mr. Taber nodded. "I recognize the wisdom of this move, and I believe it might work. If the only motive for wishing you dead is to gain possession of the estate—have it revert to the family—then telling them you have willed it to someone else will give them second thoughts. I'll have this will prepared while you wait. I think it should be done at once."

"I'd appreciate it," I said.

He called his clerk and dictated a brief will that sounded foolproof to me. While it was being run through the typewriter, Mr. Taber and I talked further.

"I have some opinions about that family, Amy. They are not very nice. It's true the deaths of Merv, Ben, and Alex do seem like murder . . ."

"I hope to prove it in the case of Alex," I said. "I have sent for a man from New York who swears he saw Alex thrown from his horse after some sort of trap caused the horse to fall. A man went up to Alex while he lay unconscious and struck him with a club. The police believed the wound had been caused by the fall."

"Amy, if this man makes an identification, it's going to create a lot of trouble. I know you won't mind that, but you'd best let me in on all the details so I can be ready to act."

"I will keep you informed," I said. "What's wrong with that family?"

"The usual, simple word describes them. They are greedy. To them the farm and winning the Cumberland are the most vital things in their lives. And I'll say this. Veronica is a changed woman since she married Gordon. I believe she married him for the moral support he offered her and apparently did not provide. Gordon, on the other hand, coveted her money and the farm."

"It's sad watching her drink herself to death."

"I have a theory about that too. If you swear never to repeat what I say, I'll tell you."

"You have my word, Mr. Taber."

"I think she drinks like that because"—he took a long breath—"she thinks that Gordon murdered her sons. The first two at least, for that's when she began drinking."

"Oh, Mr. Taber, that's a terrible thing to say."

"I agree, but that is what I have theorized. There is no other reason for her to have changed that way. Gordon doesn't abuse her. In fact, he tries to be kind to her, but she drinks herself into a state of near unconsciousness too often not to have a strong reason for doing so. She never drank before she married Gordon. She's trying to shut everything out."

I sat back, my body going limp. "There is a chance you're right. I never thought of that. Do you believe Gordon is behind this scheme to kill me?"

"He could be. The man is possessed with the dread of losing the farm."

"And the Cumberland?"

"Yes, of course. They say his horse won last year because he saw to it that Jess Foster's entry was eliminated."

"What of Len?"

"I don't know. All he lives for are those horses. I might have suspected him until you just told me whoever tried to kill you almost killed your horse as well. I cannot, no matter what the reason, see Len harming a horse, let alone trying to shoot it to death. Unless it was a horse gone amok."

"What of our jockey?"

"Carl? He is a fine example of evil. He would strangle his grandmother if there was more than two dollars in it. He's a fine jockey. One of the very best, and he counts on that to get himself out of trouble. And even while racing, other jockeys regard him as someone who would do his best to bump the other jockeys off their horses to get them dusted off by making them press too close to the rail. He's a smart one. I'd like to see him in jail."

We talked further about more minor matters and then the will was ready. I signed it, Mr. Taber provided the necessary witnesses, and he gave me a copy, ordering the original to be locked in his safe.

On my way back I stopped at the railroad station and inquired about trains from New York. There would be one early in the evening.

"Did Carl Terrell send a telegram in my name?" I asked the station agent.

"Yes, ma'am. It went right off to someone named Hugo if I remember rightly."

I thanked him, returned to the buggy, and drove home. It was midafternoon when I turned the buggy over to a hostler and went on into the house. I had asked the hostler to send Len and Carl to the house at once. I then summoned Gordon, Judith, and a somewhat bleary-eyed Veronica into the drawing room. When Len and Carl arrived, puzzled at being asked here, we all sat down. I placed the newly attested will on a table.

"As you know, there have been attempts on my live. Marion was killed. I've been shot at. I live in fear that next time a murderer will succeed. I have also reasoned that the motive for this is to be rid of me so the farm can go on and be controlled by the family. No"—I held up my hand to stop questions—"I do not believe for one instance that you are all in league to do this, but one of you may be responsible. I don't know. I cannot be sure. However, I felt that if I removed this reason for killing me, the attempts would stop. So I have just had Mr. Taber draw up a will in which I leave everything—with no exceptions—to Jess Foster. If I die, none of you will profit. I believe the will is legal and will hold, especially if there is suspicion of murder concerning my death. I'm sorry to do this, but it seems to be the only way I can protect myself."

Veronica arose abruptly and left. I knew she was going to her room to lose herself in an alcoholic haze. I was sorry to have done this to her, but there was no alternative.

Carl said, "What's it got to do with me? I ain't a member of this family."

"You work here and you have some reason," I said.

Gordon arose and went to his cigar box on the mantel. He prepared a cigar, lit it, and sat down again.

"I'm flabbergasted," he said. "You may have turned over this farm to the very man who has your death in mind. I don't trust Jess too far."

"I do," Judith said promptly. "I think Amy has done a wise thing. I hope it works out that way."

Len arose and shrugged. "Don't mean much to me. All I want is the right to care for the horses. You got nothing more to say, Amy, I'll go back and doctor Gracie some more. She's still all shook up."

He and Carl left to return to the stables. Gordon sat there filling the room with cigar smoke. I wondered if the ferocity with which he puffed on the cigar meant that he was a worried man. Perhaps disappointed would be the better word. I tried to visualize him as a man who would kill three wonderful young men just to get his hands on this farm. Mr. Taber had only been theorizing. I prayed that he was wrong.

Gordon eyed me somewhat coldly. "I'm going to ask one favor of you, Amy. Now this is your farm and you have the last word. I wish that you would put a complete stop to this business until after the Cumberland. We must win. We need the money. And we need the fame and the stud fees Valiant will bring."

I was on the verge of asking about the horse being timed in the dead of night, but Jess and I were going to solve that one ourselves.

"Gordon, I cannot do what you ask. It's impossible. Sometime tonight Pauley, the man from New

York, will arrive to try and identify whoever killed Alex. Besides that, Sheriff Lambert will be in and out, if I guess correctly. There can be no stop to this until a murderer is pointed out and arrested."

"I see. One thing more. The day after the Cumberland win or lose, I shall remove myself from this farm. I will no longer have anything to do with the place. I shall take Veronica with me, if she will come. If not, I will go anyway. I believe that concludes this talk."

He walked out, leaving a trail of smoke behind him. Judy wagged her head.

"Don't you believe him. He's talking big because he's either scared or wants to put his foot down so you'll take him more seriously. You couldn't blast him out of here with a keg of gunpowder. That also goes for Len."

"And what will happen if either one is pointed out as the man who killed Alex?"

"I don't know. My mind doesn't operate that deeply. But whatever happens, I'm on your side. I hope you believe that."

"Yes," I said, "I do. Has it ever occurred to you that perhaps Gordon, in his obsession to own this farm, may have caused the deaths of Veronica's three sons?"

Judy was startled speechless for a time. "Amy, what a thing to say!"

"I know, but there has to be some reason why Veronica is drinking herself to death. She has reason if she believes that."

"No," she said. "No, Amy. Gordon is a cunning, sly man who would happily cheat in business. He might connive to get possession of the farm, but not to the extent to do murder. I cannot believe this. I never will."

"I suppose you're right," I said. "We'll bury that idea and never bring it up again."

"Unless," Judy pointed out, "this man from New York..."

"Judy, was Gordon away from the farm at the time of Alex's death?" I shot the question at her.

"Yes. He was on a business trip to Raleigh. Len wasn't here either. He was setting up things for the Cumberland, even that far ahead, and he was in Kentucky for several days."

"Why didn't you tell me when I asked you in New York?"

"I had agreed not to. We were angry with you. We thought we were protecting ourselves and we all had to join together. Forgive me, Amy."

I nodded slowly, trying not to allow suspicion and anger to influence me. "It's strange, Judy, but even while you were so outwardly antagonistic to me, I trusted you and I liked you. I know I have not been mistaken. I want you to realize that. And now that I've disrupted the family, I think I'd better get to bed early. I'm tired."

9

There was a restlessness in me that would not be denied. I walked the floor of my parlor room. I took a warm bath. I tried looking out the window at nothing but darkness. Reading was out of the question.

I wished with all my heart that I had not agreed to meet Jess at one in the morning to try and find a horse that may not even exist. I dared not go to bed. If I had given in to the weariness that held me in a tight grip, I would have fallen asleep in seconds and never awakened. I could not even set the alarm clock, for when it went off it might awaken others who would wonder where I was bound for in the middle of the night.

So I sat for a while, paced the floor again, trying vainly to keep all these thoughts out of my mind. Predominantly I thought about that awful man from New York. He should have arrived in town early in the evening at the latest. Of course, I didn't wonder why he hadn't hired a rig and driven out to the farm. The city man might not even know how to handle a horse, let alone find his way in strange country in darkness.

I hoped that he had found some kind of accommodation and that he would arrive at the farm in the morning. Which meant I'd be unable to sleep late, so I hoped that the expedition Jess and I planned would not take too long.

When it came time for me to leave the house, everyone was in bed and, hopefully, asleep. I was as quiet as possible and managed to close the front door silently so that nobody would be disturbed. I realized I should have provided myself with a lantern, but it was too late for that now.

Moving about the area near the stables was the most difficult of all. The horses would respond to almost any alien sound, and no doubt Carl was a light sleeper, easily aroused by any strange activity by the horses. Sometimes Len, too, slept in one of the lofts. What Jess and I had to do must be under strict secrecy, for if we failed this time, there wouldn't be another.

Jess was waiting for me at the appointed place. As I approached him, I thought he was about to welcome me with outstretched arms. I saw his arms rise and then fall back. Strangely, I felt keen disappointment, though I knew very well that Jess had acted instinctively, without thought to my very recent widowhood.

"Did you get away with it?" he asked.

"I think so. Nobody awakened that I know of. How are we going to do this, Jess?"

"There's only one way. We have to prowl through the stalls until we find a likely-looking subject, which means a thoroughbred I haven't seen around here before."

"There is also a statue of Valiant," I said. "I know the barn where that is kept."

"The statue is already at Churchill Downs and publicity is being circulated about the horse. It's not a bad scheme."

"But if they are going to race Valiant, what value is this mystery horse?"

"The statue will create the kind of publicity that will cause people to remember well the last race, which Valiant won. They'll bet on him, heavily. Meantime, this horse, which is already entered, of course, will be just another horse, qualifying, but still unknown. Gordon and the others will bet on this horse, which they believe will beat Valiant. They can make a fortune on a situation like this."

"What of your entry then, Jess?"

"I've a good horse. A very good one that I believe can beat Valiant, and I intend to bet heavily on him. But if another horse runs away with the race, it's not going to be good for me or your farm, financially. Still, raising and training thoroughbreds is a gamble based on faith, and you have to carry it all the way to the track. Shall we begin now?"

He lit a storm lantern that I hadn't seen on the ground near the track gate. With this type of lantern he could shade the light and keep it from shining in every direction. We made our way down to the stables, where we stopped for two or three minutes to stand in silence, listening for any movement.

When we were sure we were still undetected, we began to enter the stables and briefly examine the horses. We found nothing unusual. Jess knew many of the thoroughbreds. Fortunately we were quiet and unobtrusive enough not to startle any of the horses. There was a whinny or two, but that often happened when no one was about, and it was not apt to arouse anyone.

Jess whispered with his lips close to my ear. "We may be wasting time this way. They wouldn't keep such a horse with the others, for fear of having it noticed. There must be a separate stall, likely the only one in that stable."

"Jess, if they moved the statue of Valiant, perhaps they put the strange horse there for the time being."

"It's possible and worth a look. They'll have to ship Valiant out soon, and the secret horse as well.

The race day is coming up fast. Everything is ready at Cumberland and we expect this to be the best-attended race since they began."

We walked softly straight for the barn where the statue of Valiant had been housed. Even before we opened the door, we heard the movements of a horse inside. Jess pulled the door open and I prayed it would not squeak and squeal as so many of them did. This one was soundless.

Jess caressed the muzzle of a somewhat restless animal. He trained the ray of the lantern and whistled softly.

"It's a brown stallion. Look at that chest! I've not seen one as strong-looking and as deep in a long time."

"It's a beautiful animal," I agreed.

He bent and ran his hands down the long legs and he exhaled sharply in surprise. He straightened up and talked in a whisper.

"Those are the legs of a thoroughbred that could win. They're muscular and long, for great strides and speed. Amy, I want to time this horse over the track."

"But how?" I protested. "You're bound to wake people up."

"Perhaps, but so much rides on this that I ask again. I beg of you, let me run this horse over the track tonight. Now! If it wakens everyone, then we have to risk that, but I must know what this horse can do. If it can beat mine, I'll not bet as heavily. It could spell the difference between going broke or staying even."

"Presumably," I said, "I am the owner of this horse. At least it is on my property and there is nothing to show it does not belong to me. You have my permission, Jess. And I don't care if the whole household is awakened. I regard this as a nasty trick, even if it is my horse and could win all that money for me. I've no idea what the purse is."

"It's respectable, sort of. But the real money is from betting. Hold the lantern, please. There's a saddle on the feed box. I have a stopwatch. Do you know how to use it?"

"I think so. You did come prepared, didn't you?"

"I suppose so. I've been very suspicious of this ever since you told me they ran a horse in the middle of the night. We'll now see."

He lifted the saddle, and the horse accepted it without any undue fuss. I walked beside Jess as he led the horse out of the barn, down to the track gate.

Inside the track I took charge of the lantern and the stopwatch. Jess was to round the track once, and as he passed me for the second time around, I was to clock the speed.

So far no lights appeared anywhere. Perhaps we'd get away with this, though I rather thought not. That horse running in the middle of the night had awakened me. Likely it had awakened others too, but they knew what it meant and would have gone back to sleep.

Jess mounted and rode off. There wasn't much noise until he began to pass me and I started the watch. The pounding of the hooves seemed very loud to me, but there was no help for it. As I understood Jess, he had to know what the chances were of this horse winning the Cumberland. And I also wanted to know, for I was determined not to be part of this kind of chicanery.

He pounded by me again and I checked the watch. After rounding the track, Jess slowed the horse, turned him, and rode back at a trot. While I waited for him, I saw a lamp lit in the loft where Carl slept, and then I heard voices from the area near the stables and I knew Len, too, had been awakened.

Jess dismounted and rubbed the horse's muzzle. The animal wasn't even breathing hard. Jess studied the watch I handed him. He whistled in surprise.

"I don't know where this horse came from, but it was from a sire and a mare both of which must have had great records. This horse is going to win. He clocked two minutes ten seconds on this track."

"We haven't won our attempt to be secret about this," I warned. "Carl and Len are awake and I think I see a light in one of the upstairs windows of the mansion."

"We'll have to face it out," Jess said. "They can't accuse us of trying to cheat on them. I only hope it doesn't mean a great deal of trouble for you."

"You forget, Jess, I own everything here. Unless there are papers to show this horse belongs to someone else, he's mine too. And if such papers do show up, someone has to pay this farm for training and keeping the horse. Under the circumstances, I'm not afraid of them. That is—not much. I do recall what has happened, however, and I'll be careful."

Carl and Len reached us first. By then Jess was perched on the track rail and I stood beside him.

"What you have done, Amy, is the most dastardly thing I've ever known," Len said angrily. "And you, Jess, ought to be ashamed of yourself. If this animal has been injured..."

"I'm going to find out," Carl said.

I said, "What is so dastardly about running my own horse? Even in the middle of the night. Even if I never saw the animal before. It is my horse."

"Like hell it is," Carl shouted.

"Oh," I exclaimed. "Explain then how it happens the horse is on my property, has been here for some time, has been raised and fed here, raced in the middle of the night too. No one asked my permission to allow this."

"I gave Carl permission," Len said. "It's his horse."

"He'd better have the papers to prove it," Jess said.

"You keep out of this," Len retorted angrily. "We never wanted you around here anyway."

"I can sure see why," Jess said.

"Len," I said, "this is not your farm. You had no right to give permission for anything. If Carl cannot prove this horse is his, by producing authentic papers, I will claim the animal. If he does show them, I shall demand payment—very generously—for using my property in training the horse. If it is not paid by track time, I shall prevent the running of the horse. Do you quite understand that?"

Len's face, shadowed by the ray of the lanterns now placed on the ground, seemed like the face of a man I didn't know. It was filled with a rage that wasn't going to be held back much longer and might explode into something so violent we'd not be able to handle him. I had to cool him down.

"I will leave obtaining of this proof up to you, Len, and I hope everything works out for you and Carl."

Jess, too, realized Len's anger had to be abated. "I'll say this, it's the best horse I've ridden in my life. And the fastest."

"It's the best horse in the world. The best-trained and he can win any race at any track. He's worth a fortune."

"The horse wasn't hurt any," Carl called out. "If he had been, I'd have killed you, Jess."

I said, "Carl, you will pack your things and leave this farm by noon tomorrow. If this is your horse, you may take him with you, but I do not wish a jockey like you to wear the colors of my farm. In other words, you're fired."

"I wasn't going to ride Valiant anyway," Carl said. "That big brute ain't got a chance. And yours will be lucky he comes in third place, Jess."

Jess didn't comment. The atmosphere was still ready to explode if the wrong thing was said. Carl led the horse back to the stables. Len, still grumbling, left us, and we walked slowly back to the mansion, which was, by now, all lit up, though no one had emerged.

Gordon was seated in the drawing room, a long purple robe around him. Judy was there too, in a negligee. Veronica was nowhere about. I expected no sound short of a cannon could have awakened her.

Gordon said, "So now you know."

"Yes," I said. "We know. Why wasn't I told?"

"You're much too honest," Judy said. "You'd never have gone along with it."

"So you knew too," I said in a voice tinged with disappointment. "I thought you and I were on the same side, Judy."

"We are, Amy. If you'll only realize that Greenlawn Farm is successful but not too profitable. Its success in breeding and raising fine horses is well-known, but even with this reputation the farm does not do that well."

"We will be set up for life if this idea works," Gordon said. "I've bet everything I own on Carl's horse."

"Does it really belong to Carl?" Jess asked.

"You can't prove otherwise," Gordon replied.

"What you're saying is that this horse is Amy's property, but she can't prove it," Jess commented.

"Mind your own business, Jess," Gordon warned. "We accepted you because that's what Amy wanted, but we don't have to keep considering you as a friend. Especially since you were an enemy for so many months."

"Stop it," I said.

"One more word," Jess said. "If Carl owns this horse, there have to be records of it at the track or the horse can't run. Perhaps we can't prove this horse belongs to Amy, but it's possible we can prove the papers registering the animal are fraudulent. Have you thought of that, Gordon?"

"The papers are in order. You'll not come up with any evidence otherwise...."

"Not before the race, of course. Time is too limited for that, but later . . . perhaps . . ."

I stood up. "We've had enough of this for tonight. In the morning we'll take it up again and this time we'll see how it relates to any attempt to murder me, and the actual killing of my best friend. It comes to a point where neither Carl's horse nor Valiant may run in the Cumberland."

Judy turned her back on me and went up to her room. Gordon lit a fresh cigar and seemed to be settled in the drawing room for the rest of the night. I took Jess by the arm and led him out onto the veranda.

"It's a mess," I said. "I don't know how to handle this, or what to do about it. But tomorrow Pauley is coming from the town and what he says, or does, may settle the whole thing. If Marion was killed because she'd been mistaken for me and it was meant that I should have been kicked to death by that mad horse, then everything is off. I'll allow no entry from this farm in the Cumberland and I shall see to it that whoever is responsible for all these deaths, and this violence, is faced with the kind of justice he deserves."

"I don't like you being in that house alone

tonight. Gordon is in a rage even if he doesn't show it as much as Len. If they were ever involved in what happened to Marion, they could be dangerous. Carl is the worst. He hasn't the intellect to know when to stop. And you can be assured, Len won't try to keep him quiet."

"I'm terribly disappointed in Len," I said.

"You have to understand that Len's entire life has been concerned with raising and breeding thoroughbreds. And all that work leads to only one thing—winning races, especially the Cumberland. In my opinion there is nothing Len wouldn't do to bring in a winner."

"Including murder?" I asked.

"Even that. Provided he thought he could get away with it. Carl is different. He's a hothead who acts without reason. Other jockeys consider him as a very dangerous man to race against. He's a master at tricks and has pulled them all. He's been responsible, so they say, for injury to several riders. I wouldn't trust him."

"He'll be gone tomorrow," I said. "Or I shall take legal steps to see that he leaves. I'm angry too, Jess. Len, Gordon, and Carl may go into rages, but I'm not up to that. However, don't think I'm going to stand by and let all this happen without taking some kind of action."

"My opinion is that the horse was foaled right here on Greenlawn and everybody knows it," Jess said. "His sire could even be Valiant's and there are several fine brood mares here to add to this horse's heritage. If Carl owns this animal and bought it somewhere else, he'd not have trained it here or offered to share the profits of this horse with anyone. He's not the kind to share. I'm sure he does not own the horse."

"What can we do?" I asked. "There's so little time."

"I hate to leave you at this moment," he said, "but I think I'd best go to Cumberland in the morning and investigate Carl's claim of ownership. Any papers he presented have to be faked, and I'll try to prove that. If I can, then the ownership of this horse will surely revert to you."

"Don't worry about me," I assured him,. "I'll be all right."

"You've more confidence in these people than I have. Remember Marion. Ask me to stay and I will. Let Carl win the race if he can, and prove him a thief afterward."

"I'd rather you proved he is not the owner now, before the race," I said. "I promise to be very careful."

"All right. I'll be on my way early in the morning. It shouldn't take too long and I'll come right back. Please, Amy, watch out. I'll meet you at the track if possible."

"I'll look forward to it," I said.

He leaned forward and kissed me on the lips before he walked abruptly off the veranda and hurried to where he'd left his horse. I heard him ride into the night before I turned back to the house.

No one was about, not even Gordon, when I entered, I went up to bed after extinguishing the gas lamps in the drawing room and the reception hall. In my own room I prepared for bed, but as I blew out the lamp, I thought I heard movement outside. I went to the window quickly, drew aside the curtain, and peered into the night. I saw a dim form, on horseback, slowly patrolling the area around the house.

I recognized Jess instantly and I pressed my face against the coolness of the windowpane. He was in love with me and there was a growing feeling within me that I could easily fall in love with him. Only the fond memory of another man I loved kept me from admitting it to myself and doing something about it.

10

As Lena set my breakfast plate before me, she bent down to whisper. "That man Carl, he rode out o' here 'bout five in the mornin'. Reckon he cleared out finally?"

"I hope so," I said. "I ordered him off the farm."

"Sure didn't leave empty-handed. I saw him lead a likely-looking horse as he rode away."

"He claims he owns that horse, Lena. I don't think he does, but I can't prove it, so I don't know how I could have stopped him."

"He's no good, Miss Amy. Never did have a right to be here all the time. Mr. Alex shooed him away more'n once."

"Is Len still here? Or has he left for Cumberland already?"

"He's here. Had his breakfast early like always, but sure didn't have much to say. Acted to me like a man mighty mad at the world."

"He had reason to be."

Lena went off to fetch a pot of hot coffee and I ate my breakfast alone, occupied with so many conflicting thoughts and ideas that I felt dizzy.

Judith came down before I finished and Lena served her. Judy didn't speak until I was about ready to get up and leave the table.

"I wouldn't have expected that of you, Amy," she said.

"Expected what? That I refused to allow Carl's horse to run unless he proved ownership?"

"Amy, what difference does it make who owns the animal? Majesty will win and all the glory will come to our farm. Your farm."

"So Majesty is the name of the horse," I said. "I'd have thought he'd be named Midnight after the time when his training was done."

"Long before you got here that horse was being trained. We had to suspend it after you arrived because we were afraid you'd not consent to Gordon's idea on how to make the farm wealthy."

"If you mean touting Valiant as the horse to bet on and even causing a statue of that horse to be set up at the track so all would be reminded what a great horse he is, then I say that's fraud the moment you plan to run Majesty. Because you are the only ones who know Majesty will win. I do not countenance trickery, Judy, and I'm surprised that you do."

"Are you now?" Judy placed her knife and fork on the plate. "You never grew up on a farm like this. Where the only product is fine horseflesh. Yes, we sell all kinds of horses for all sorts of purposes, but the main one is to win races with one of the animals. Winning the Cumberland and the other big races is the difference between success and failure. Between security and bankruptcy."

"Are you telling me that if I stop Carl from running that horse we'll go broke?"

"Practically so. But with Valiant and Majesty at stud we can grow rich. Or you can. I keep thinking the farm still belongs to the family and not you alone."

"Is it planned then that if Carl wins with Majesty, it will then be revealed that the horse is Greenlawn property?"

"No—but Greenlawn will arrange to buy the animal."

"And what we pay will be Carl's portion of this game?"

"I don't know. Gordon handles that."

"Suppose I say fine, that's wonderful. Race the horse as you see fit, and win. That's the most important thing. Win! What did Alex win, Judy? What were the shares given to Ben and Merv—and Marion? Don't forget Marion. There has been murder. Several times over. In the case of murder, Judy, nothing rises above that in the importance of knowing who killed those people."

"The main purpose is to win. The rest of it can be settled afterward."

"Have you given a thought that for me there may not be an afterward? Have you forgotten that my own life has been threatened?"

"I can't talk to you." Judith arose abruptly and angrily from the table. "You will not even try to understand. I'm sorry for you, Amy, because you are going to lose this farm. We'll all suffer from that, including Alex's mother. We're all going to the track today. We can't stop you from going with us, but for my part, I'd rather not be with you."

"I'm sorry," I said, but she fled from the room and ran upstairs. I left the table too and went into the drawing room, where I sat down to consider the situation, to think about the ideas Judy used to persuade me. I knew she was wrong and I was right. The coming race actually might mean the failure of Greenlawn, but I was prepared for that. I went into the library and opened the books. My experience let me learn promptly that while Greenlawn had been financially sound, Gordon had, without my permission, bet an enormous amount of money on Carl's horse. I suppose the money was bet in an assortment of names, but it was bet, or would be just before the race began. There could be a killing made from this plan, but I still refused to go along with it. Under no circumstances would I favor something that had already resulted in multiple murders.

Gordon came down to add his pleading to Judy's. It was easier to deny him because, after Judy, my mind was firmly made up and nothing was going to change it.

"I'm going to be calm about this," he said. "But what I have to say is in the form of a warning. If you stop Carl from racing that horse, I fully expect he will kill you."

"Perhaps as he killed all the others?" I asked. "I'm going to try and prove he did, and if I do, Gordon, Carl will be in no position to harm anyone. I'm not afraid of him."

"Well, you've been warned."

"From what you say he must have murdered Marion, believing it was me he killed. You should have expressed this opinion long ago. I will not change my mind no matter what the consequences may be."

"It could all be so easy. . . ." he began in a pleading voice.

"No!" I said firmly.

He arose in anger and stalked out of the drawing room. Len brought the carriage around. I'd not been invited to accompany them to the track. I would not have gone anyway. I was waiting for the man from New York to arrive. Having him disclose who had killed Alex was of more importance to me than watching a race won or lost.

Jess hadn't returned, but naturally with his own entry he'd be a busy man. I went upstairs to my room. Except for Jess, all I had now were enemies. They'd never forgive me if their plans fell through,

BRIDAL BLACK

which they surely would if Jess's mission had been successful in proving that Carl had entered a horse under false papers.

Presently they all gathered their baggage and assembled in the reception hall. Len, Gordon, and Judith waited in an uncomfortable silence until Veronica came down, the last of the family to be ready. Gordon began carrying the bags to the waiting carriage.

Veronica, who had been dragooned into going along, was ill-at-ease, nervous, and likely in need of a drink.

"I forgot," she said. "It does get chilly in Cumberland and we do go about at night. I'll need my fur wrap."

"It's in the attic cedar closet," Judith said impatiently. "We're in a hurry."

"But I do need it," she persisted, and defying them, she turned and began to climb the stairs. I knew about the attic cedar closet. It was a very large, supposedly mothproof vault where furs were stored. It was also very dark and dismal. I doubted Veronica could find what she wanted. I followed her up the stairs, down the corridor between the bedrooms.

She suddenly turned back and passed by me. "I also forgot my smelling salts," she explained. "I do need them."

We both entered her suite of rooms and I stood by while she ferreted through the various bottles and jars on her bureau, until she found the lavender-scented smelling salts. She tucked this into her handbag. We then resumed our way to the attic.

The stairs, at the end of the corridor, were very narrow, very steep, and quite treacherous. That was another reason I'd accompanied her. I was afraid she might fall.

The attic was dimly lit by two cobwebbed, quite

dirty fan windows at each end of it. Boxes, barrels, and old trunks were placed at random, making it necessary to weave our way to the cedar closet at the end of the attic. I preceded Veronica, raised the heavy brass latch, and braced myself to pull open the rather thick door. I was about to turn around and move aside so Veronica could enter the quite dark room and make her own selection of the furs that were stored there.

Someone clapped a hand to the small of my back and gave me a vicious, strong push that actually hurled me into the closet. I struck the opposite wall with a painful impact that sent me to my knees. Before I could get up, the door was slammed shut and I was enveloped in an absolute darkness.

I got to my feet, pushed aside some of the furs that encumbered my way to the door. I tried to open it, but the door had been secured on the outside by the heavy latch. There was no inside provision for raising the latch. I was locked in.

For a few seconds the impact didn't strike me. I banged on the door and called out to be set free. Then it came to me that I was locked in here by deliberate intent to keep me away from the track.

I was still reeling a bit from my collision with the wall, so I sat down. The only place I could sit was on the floor. I wondered how long they intended to keep me here in the stygian darkness. If their intentions were to make me a prisoner until they returned, then I was in a desperate situation. They'd be gone for at least two, if not three days. I'd be in here without water or food. It was already growing unbearably hot in this confined space, for the whole attic had been quite warm.

I tried to orient my thoughts. I wondered if this came about with Veronica's help. If she had demanded permission to fetch her furs from the cedar closet and hoped I would accompany her, then she was involved. Or, if I did not, she might have asked my help. Certainly whoever had delivered me into this hot box had not been Veronica. Not unless she had acquired far more strength than I knew she had. On the contrary, she was given to leaning on me whenever we walked together.

So someone had either been hidden in the attic, which would be proof that Veronica was part of the scheme, or someone had preceded us to the attic after Veronica had insisted on going there. It could be nothing except a plan coming out of the blue and enacted on the spur of the moment by someone other than Veronica. That meant Len, Gordon, or Judith. I discounted Judith and Gordon for they had gone out of the house with the luggage. So that left Len alone to take advantage of an unplanned situation. I recalled how Veronica had stopped by her bedroom to fetch her smelling salts. In those few seconds, Len could have moved quickly and silently along the corridor to precede us to the attic, concealed himself, and at the auspicious moment when I had opened the door, pushed me inside and closed the door before I could even turn about and see who was responsible.

If Veronica made any objections to this, Len could have silenced her, even overpowered her, and taken her downstairs. By now they were all aboard the carriage and on their way to the railroad station and Cumberland, while I sweated and worried myself into a near frenzy in the silent darkness of this vault.

I forced myself to be calm. The best thing to do was move slowly, exert as little energy as possible, and try to find something with which I might be able to force my way out.

I prowled about in the dark, impeded by the furs and half-smothered by them, and searched the rack on which they hung for some metallic object that might help me escape.

Then I remembered that this was no ordinary lock. It was all on the outside. There was no keyhole through which I might try to manipulate the lock. I sat down again. By this time I began to realize that there was no possible way out unless someone raised the latch. I was doomed to remain here until they returned.

I had no means of knowing the passage of time. It did seem I'd been in this vault about two hours, possibly a bit more, and my anxiety was beginning to lead to terror. I'd tried to determine, in my mind, who might come by. Certainly none of the family would return. It was to their advantage that I remained locked in this tomb. Jess was at the track, probably prepared to meet the train, hoping I'd be on it. Every servant in the house had long since left for the track. The Cumberland Stakes was one celebration no one missed. The high and the low all attended.

I was alone in the house. A prisoner in my own home. There was no chance of release. How I'd be able to endure this confinement for days, without going insane, was something I'd have to contend with. I had to keep my wits about me and never surrender to terror.

It was some time later, perhaps about another half-hour, when I realized I was breathing much oftener than usual and my breaths were extended, like someone seeking more oxygen. It was then that all my plans to remain calm were shattered.

This was an airtight vault. Not a chink of light showed below, above, or at the side of the door. The vault was meant to keep out insects and too much air. I was slowly being suffocated. The only thing that had saved me was the size of the vault.

I got up and began to pound on the door, to kick at it, and to scream. There was no longer need to be concerned about how I would endure this confinement until the family returned. My problem was to stay alive during the next two or three hours.

Realizing that too much activity, too much screaming, not only did me little good, but also utilized oxygen so precious to the maintenance of my life, I sat down again and this time I lowered my head and began to cry. It was awful, giving in to my fears like this, but there was no help for it. I was at the end of my resources. In a matter of a short time—an hour, perhaps only minutes—I'd be dead. As surely as if someone had pressed a pillow against my face to cut off air to my lungs.

I felt myself growing dizzy. When I tried to move, it required a considerable effort. The best thing I could do was be quiet. I was going to die anyway, so I might as well prolong my life a few more minutes, if I could. There was always hope, so I'd been told over and over again since I was a child. But locked in here, alone, no way out and no rescue possible as far as I could determine, there was no longer any hope. A lassitude began to envelop me. I could only sit here with my back against the wall, with furs sometimes gently brushing my back and shoulders. It would be over soon, I knew. And the sooner the better, my mind told me pessimistically, though I was still going to fight for my life. That is, if there was anything to fight with.

I heard it dimly. I couldn't make out what the sound was at first, but then it did seem like a human voice far, far away. I managed to get to my feet. It came again, this time there was no doubt of it. This was not a dying fancy. Someone was in the house.

I summoned every ounce of strength I had left. I kicked the door, I banged on it with my fists, I jumped up and down, pounding my feet against the floor. I screamed and screamed until the sound rang in my ears like the tolling of a great bell. I kept this up until my stamina rapidly was used up and then I slowly sank to the floor, with my hands still against the door and sliding down, as I did.

I was on the verge of dropping into unconsciousness when the sound was quite close this time. I managed to remove a shoe and with this I beat at the door, weakly perhaps, but it sufficed.

Suddenly my eyes ached from bright light. Actually it was only the dim light in the attic. I was staring at a pair of sturdy-looking legs encased in trousers. I tried to raise my head to see who it was. Through my mind a sluggish idea took shape: that someone had returned to make sure I was dead.

Strong hands lifted me. I was raised in someone's arms and was being carried across the attic. I could smell the odor of tobacco and my cheek rubbed gently against an unshaven one.

I knew I was being slowly carried down those treacherous stairs, then along the corridor, and finally placed gently on a bed. Someone raised a window and fresh, cool air swept in to soothe my aching lungs.

I opened my eyes finally and looked up into the worried face of Sheriff Lambert. He was trying to get me to drink water from a glass he held to my lips. I did drink, and deeply. I breathed even more deeply and I knew then that I was safe.

"How in the world did you get locked in that closet?" he asked.

"Don't know for sure," I managed to reply.

"Rest awhile," he advised. "There's no hurry. We can talk when you feel more up to it. Maybe you'd like a drink of brandy? Yes . . . I would too. It'll bring both of us around faster."

He returned in a few moments with the brandy decanter and glasses. I sipped mine and it did make me feel a little better. I was able to sit up and then to get to my feet, somewhat unsteadily at first, but with Lambert's help I made it downstairs to the drawing room.

I said, "Thank you, Sheriff. If ever you saved a life, it was certainly mine. In a few more minutes I'd have suffocated."

"You couldn't have locked yourself in there, Amy. Who did it?"

"I don't know. I was helping Veronica get her furs and someone just shoved me into the vault and slammed the door. There was no way out."

"Gordon, or Len, or even Carl. Has to be one of those."

"Carl wasn't present. He'd left for the track. I think Gordon was loading luggage into the carriage, and that leaves Len. I would not suspect that Judith either knew about it or took any part. Veronica may have wanted to tell them I was in danger, but if Len had intimidated her, she'd be silent. She never fights them, just gives in if she has a bottle to comfort her."

"She'll likely speak if we assure her she won't be harmed," he said. "That can wait. I came here on official business. I found the front door unlocked, so I walked in. I hollered to find out if anyone was here, but I got no answer. Then as I was about to leave I thought I heard the sound of something that sounded like hammering. So I began looking about. Finally I figured the noise came from the attic, so I came up here and ... you know the rest."

"I know what would have happened to me if you had not come by."

"Call it pure luck," he said.

"May I ask about the business that sent you here?

Has it to do with a man who arrived from New York last evening?"

He handed me a slip of paper on which was written my name, the name of the farm and directions on how to get here. I handed it back.

"I'm afraid to ask any more questions, Sheriff."

"Did you write this note?"

"I never saw it before. I don't know who wrote it, but I know where you found it. In the possession of a dead man. Isn't that true?"

"You're a good guesser, Amy."

"It wasn't a guess. I expected this after all else that's happened here. This man was on his way to try to identify the man who set a trap for my husband and murdered him."

"Do you know his name, where he comes from?"

"His name is Pauley. I can put you in touch with someone who can tell you more about him. He is dead, isn't he?"

"Before dawn this morning a horse, rented out with a buggy from the livery stable, came back without the buggy and somewhat injured. We set out to find the buggy and the man who rented it. We found the buggy overturned and dragged a considerable distance before the shafts broke and the horse was set free to make his way back to where he belonged. The man who had rented the buggy had been thrown clear. His neck was broken. He's dead."

"The note was on him?" I asked.

"Yes, in his pocket."

"I wrote a telegram and sent it to the depot for transmission. Carl attended that errand. The telegram was to a friend of mine who knew this dead man. I asked that he come here at once, make his way to the farm, and identify the man he says he saw murder Alex. Someone met him, Sheriff, and wrote these directions. Someone who met him again, later, and killed him."

"How do you know this, Amy?" he asked.

"Because the dead man never wrote the note. He told me he couldn't read or write a word. The man who met him wrote the note. Now my only chance of identifying whoever killed Alex is gone."

Sheriff Lambert fanned his face with his broad-brimmed hat. "This is getting to be too much for a small-town law officer like me. But I'm going to find out if this man was murdered, and if he was, I'm going to hunt for his killer as much as I'm still looking for whoever killed your friend and guest."

"Thank you," I said.

"You have a part in this as well. First of all, you will have to come to town with me and identify the dead man. And give me enough information so I can notify his people, if he has any."

"I doubt he has. To me he seemed a drifter, but I can't be sure. I'll tell you how to find out."

"The other matter is to ask you who you believe killed this man and, possibly, the others."

"Carl Terrell, the jockey employed on the farm. I fired him last night. He and everyone else, I'm afraid, are part and parcel of a fantastic scheme to make a great deal of money at the track. It's very involved. . . ."

"You can tell me on our way to town."

"As you wish. Perhaps I should saddle my horse and I can ride it back here to save you the trouble."

"A welcome idea. Shall I see to the horse?"

"Please wait. I'm not a good rider and there is only one horse that seems to realize this. I feel safe on her. I'll be ready in five or ten minutes."

I couldn't use my riding habit, for it had all but been destroyed in my frantic movements through the forest. I did have a riding skirt, however, and along with a shirtwaist and a short jacket, I was suitably dressed for riding.

The sheriff and I rode the buggy to the stables, where I brought out Gracie and the sheriff quickly saddled her. We tied her to the back of his buggy and began our grim journey. On the way I detailed the facts about the scheme hatched between Gordon, Len, and Carl. The sheriff wagged his head from side to side.

"Of all the crazy ideas I ever heard, this one beats the others. And you know, they might get away with it. That is, without interference on your part."

"Sheriff, it's my farm. It's a farm that my husband loved and that he left to me. I don't want the name of it blackened by any chicanery such as this. Gordon claims I'll lose the farm if we don't pull it off, but I'd rather that."

"I can certainly see why you believe as you do. Now I have a few things to tell you, which I've kept under my hat so far. I've not been idle since your friend from New York was killed by that crazy horse. I agree that it was murder. The blow on her head was not from any hoof pounding by a horse. The autopsy proved that. The horse finished the job, no doubt, but did not inflict that first blow. So we know it was murder. As far as I can ascertain the only person connected with this wild scheme, who was not accounted for at the time this murder took place, was Carl. So you see, I quite agree with your suspicions. There's more."

"I hope so," I said. "That's not enough to convict Carl."

"I realize that. Now you gave Carl a telegram to send to New York asking that this man come down here. Isn't that correct?"

"Yes, it is, Sheriff."

"What did you say in the telegram?"

BRIDAL BLACK 153

"I instructed an elevator operator named Hugo, who works in the New York hotel where I was employed, to reach Pauley and tell him to come at once, to ask directions in town and ride out to the farm as soon as possible. I telegraphed money for his expenses."

Sheriff Lambert sighed in exasperation. "Carl couldn't even let that go as it was. He changed the wording. I've a copy here. You may have it. Carl asked that this man come here, and when he got off the train, he would be met. I think Carl met him. I think Carl told him to go right out to the farm and gave him this note we found on him."

"Well, as I told you before," I said quickly. "The little man from New York never wrote that note himself. He told me he could neither read nor write a word."

"Good, that will help. Especially if we prove it is Carl's handwriting, which is possible. In my opinion, Carl sent him on his way, rode quickly to head him off, and when he stopped the buggy, he killed the man, tipped the buggy, and spooked the horse into running until the shafts broke. I don't know how we can prove that, but I'll try."

I accompanied Sheriff Lambert to the local mortician's, where the body had been taken. I braced myself as I was led into a room where the man from New York lay in death.

"That," I said, "is the man I know as Pauley. I don't know his full name."

"Thank you," Lambert said. "I'll get busy and have the New York police department determine who he was and what we should do with the body. I appreciate your help, Miss Amy. It's not an easy task, identifying someone under these conditions."

11

As I rode toward the house, I saw the carriage at the front of the veranda. Once again I grew filled with fear and anxiety. Someone had come back to make sure I was dead. This was the carriage they'd all gone off in. For a moment I was inclined to turn my horse around and ride back to town as fast as I could so I might summon Sheriff Lambert.

But as I considered this idea, Judy emerged from the door to stand on the veranda and wave both hands at me. I decided to take a chance. What I really wanted to hear was that Judy had come back to free me from the cedar room.

I rode up cautiously, ready to turn the horse if anyone else appeared. Judy still waved frantically and I took a chance. I rode up to the veranda stairs, but I remained on the horse.

"Thank God you're safe," she called to me. "I was scared to death I'd find you still in the storage room."

"You knew, then, that I was locked in there?"

"Veronica told us. She couldn't hold it back any longer even if she was so afraid of Len."

"Then Len locked me in?" I asked.

"Yes. Gordon didn't know about it, nor did I, until Veronica broke down and told us. Len left us as quickly as he could. We haven't seen him since."

BRIDAL BLACK 155

I dismounted and walked up the steps to the veranda. "Thank you, Judy."

She embraced me quickly. "Amy, please believe me. We did not know. Len acts as if he's gone crazy. All he wants is for that horse to win and Carl is going to ride him tomorrow. That's all they think about, Gordon and Len. Win the race. Never mind how or what happens. Just win it. Lots of horse breeders are like that. They live for nothing else. I love the races and I want our horse to win, but not that much."

"I wanted so much to know you had nothing to do with this, Judy. Thank you for coming back."

"I don't know how it all happened. Veronica says you accompanied her to the attic, as I knew you did. Len just took advantage of a situation that developed unexpectedly. After he locked you in the closet, he seized Veronica and forced her downstairs. He told her that if she said anything about what happened he'd kill her just as he killed all the others."

"All the others?" I asked. "Does that mean Ben, Merv, Alex . . . ?"

"I don't know. Len frightened her so she was afraid to say a word until he went off somewhere and then she couldn't stand it any longer. Len came back and was furious when he found out Veronica had told us. He left very hurriedly. Gordon told me to hurry back and set you free—if I wasn't too late."

"You would have been," I told her. "Sheriff Lambert came by looking for me. The man from New York arrived last night—and he was murdered. Sheriff Lambert believes Carl did that."

Judy nodded slowly. "It does seem that Carl and Len are in this together. I'd never considered that before. In fact, I never considered anything. I didn't realize it before, even though I never trusted Carl.

But Len . . . he was always so kind and gentle. He loves horses more than his own life."

"But why should he have killed the three brothers? He was content here, or he seemed to be."

"I think Len can't stand supervision. Merv and Ben used to order him about and sometimes disregarded his suggestions even if they were good. Alex was different. He let Len run the training part of the farm. But I suppose Len believed that if he got rid of the brothers he would have his own way all the time. Gordon is interested only in the business end. Or perhaps Len planned to eventually gain complete control of the farm."

"By killing everyone?" I asked, aghast at the idea.

"How can I answer that? But if he did kill the brothers and knew Carl killed Marion—and now this man from New York—he must be a madman."

"I wonder what he'll do when he's accused of these crimes," I said.

"Whatever charges are made will have to be proven, Amy. How can that be done?"

"I'm not sure. You told me that when Alex was killed in New York, Len wasn't here."

"Yes, I can swear to that, and Carl was not here either when it happened; he could have been responsible."

"It's all going to come out now," I assured her. "Sheriff Lambert is working on it and we know enough to assure Len's arrest. Carl's as well."

"I'm glad it's about over," Judy said. "And I'm thoroughly ashamed of myself for the way I acted toward you. Now if we want to be at the track when the race begins, we'd better get ready to leave now. There's a night train but it's a short ride over the border. I'm sure we can rest a bit before the track opens."

"I'll put up Gracie," I said. "And we'll use the carriage to go to the railroad station. I want to change too. I'll be as fast as I can. Tell me, did you see Jess?"

"When I first arrived. You know, Amy, I could have fallen in love with him so easily. I know now how futile that would have been."

"Why futile?" I asked with some trepidation.

"Oh, Amy, he's in love with you. Don't you know that?"

"Yes, I suppose I do."

"If you're hesitating because Alex hasn't been dead long, I think you're making a mistake. You have your own life to live. Alex is gone. Keep his memory alive, yes, but don't attach yourself to his memory forever. He'd want you to be happy, and if Jess can make you happy, then go to him."

I didn't reply, but I untied Gracie from the hitchrack, mounted her, and rode off slowly, heading for the stables. It would take but a few minutes to water and feed her, go back to the house, dress and pack a few things, and Judy and I would be on our way.

I felt free of worry and fear for the first time in days. Everything was coming to an end soon. Carl would likely be arrested after the race. Len seemed to have already fled after Veronica found the courage to tell how I'd been locked in the cedar closet. In the morning I'd be with Jess. I intended to stay with him until the race was over, and to me it didn't matter a fig who won.

Carl, with that unusual horse, probably would come in first, and either our horse or Jess's would make it second or third. Yet the race, so vital to everyone else, was like an aftermath to me.

I began pulling up, ready to dismount. Suddenly there was Len, astride a huge stallion. He'd ridden around the corner of one stable. In one hand he held a pitchfork. I could see the tines gleam in the afternoon sunlight and the weapon was poised to kill me.

"Len," I said, "it will do you no good...."

"You little bitch," he yelled, and his voice had the strident tones of someone more than a little mad.

"Len... please..."

He was urging his horse forward, not yet into a trot, but I knew that within seconds he would send that horse into a charge that would run me down before I could turn Gracie and try to outride him. An impossibility in any event.

Len dug heels into his horse and the animal broke into that charge I expected. But knowing it would come, I was at least somewhat prepared. I yanked at the reins and Gracie turned sharply just as Len hurled the pitchfork at me. I felt the breeze of it, but the fork missed and landed on the ground to be stuck there, the shaft of it quivering from the impact.

Len came at me, unarmed now, but fully prepared to kill me by forcing me from the saddle and then riding me down. I screamed for help. I wanted Judy to at least witness this and get away before Len could reach her.

The big stallion brushed against Gracie so hard she was thrown off balance. It was a cleverly executed maneuver, for it sent me falling out of the saddle. I landed on the turf. Behind me, about twenty feet away, was the fence to the private racetrack. If I could reach that...

But Len anticipated this move and swung his horse before I could hope to reach the fence. Now he was going to ride me down. If I turned to flee, I'd not last a dozen steps. That horse would cut me down instantly. So I faced the horse and Len, and at the last second I threw myself to one side and barely escaped the animal's hooves.

BRIDAL BLACK

I fell after I jumped, and I rolled quickly to gain my feet. I found myself about two feet from where the pitchfork was stuck in the ground. I freed it, raised the tines, and pointed them straight at the oncoming animal. If the horse reached me, it would likely be killed by the fork. It was the only defense I had and I remained steadfast, not lowering the fork. Len screamed something and veered the horse. He was watching me so closely he didn't realize he was heading straight for the fence.

His horse was not a good jumper and it suddenly balked just before it would have hit the fence. The balk, after such high speed, sent Len flying out of the saddle, over the horse's head, to clear the fence and land headfirst on the hard track. He didn't move a muscle after he hit.

Judy was running toward me, screaming at the top of her voice. Holding the pitchfork, I walked slowly to the gate, through it, and up to the spot where Len lay. Judy reached me, too horrified to speak. I nudged Len's body with my foot. He didn't respond in any way, but I was still unable to trust him. He might suddenly get up and fulfill his promise of murder.

Judy bent down and turned him over. His head fell to one side in an awful manner that showed us he had broken his neck. Death had come to him as it had to his victims.

Judy began to weep. I turned away, dry-eyed. I couldn't bring myself to weep for that man, but I was glad it ended this way. That I hadn't directly killed him. I began to walk slowly back toward Gracie and I mechanically led her to the stall, where I fed and watered her. Judy brought Len's big stallion back to the barn before she joined me.

I entered the tack room, a short distance from the stable, and procured a blanket. Judy and I returned to where Len's body lay and I covered it with a blanket. Then I gave way. Even if this man had tried to kill me, I had once regarded him with respect and affection. I went over to the fence, leaned against the rail, and wept. Perhaps it was with relief that it was over now, or perhaps I did have some compassion for a man who must have pulled up his horse at the last instant because the animal would have been impaled by that pitchfork. Len's love for horses cost him his life.

Judy's arm went around my shoulders. "He doesn't deserve your tears, Amy, but I know how you feel. We'd better get started. We can ride into town and notify Sheriff Lambert what happened. I'm sure he'll let us continue on to the track."

I nodded, but I couldn't speak. We walked back to the house in silence. Once in my room, I began to recover from the shock of what I'd been through and I was able to move about faster and think in a clearer manner. I even inspected one of the dresses that Marion had brought. An Eton suit in blue broadcloth trimmed in velvet. Stylish enough for the track, warm enough if the weather turned cool. I packed this, with whatever accessories I required, and in twenty minutes joined Judy downstairs.

We locked up the house, boarded the carriage, and drove to town. I found Sheriff Lambert in his office at the jail.

"Len returned to the house," I explained. "He tried to kill me, but he was thrown by his horse and was killed. His body lies on the racetrack at the farm. Neither Judy nor I could do anything for him. You may regard her as a witness to what happened, but I ask that we be allowed to go to Cumberland so we may see the race."

"So it was Len." The sheriff shook his head in dismay. "Always thought of him as a quiet man who lived for nothing but horses. Odd he was killed in the same way he had others killed."

"I believe he sent Carl to kill my husband," I said. "I believe he killed Merv and Ben, and he schemed with Carl to murder me. But Carl made a mistake and killed Marion instead. It was Len who locked me in the cedar closet. Veronica confessed to this, and in time so that Judy could come back and do her best to save my life."

"She wouldn't have been in time," Lambert reminded me. "You'd have been dead within an hour after I found you."

"Yes, I know, but Veronica did break down and send help. She's a confused and tortured woman, Sheriff. She did her best. I don't hold anything against her."

"We now know Carl did meet that man from New York at the depot. Two people saw them together and recognized the dead man. I've a warrant for Carl's arrest for murder. The authorities at Cumberland will pick him up right after the race."

"I'm satisfied with that," I told him. "We do hold to the importance of that race, though, don't we?"

"Allowing Carl to ride? Yes, I'm afraid we do. But he'll be watched and there will be no chance that he can get away."

"Thank you," I said.

"He's a vicious little monster, but he'll be paying for those crimes, Miss Amy. Leave that to me."

I rejoined Judy, who had stayed with the carriage. She drove to the railroad station in time to put up the carriage and the horse and meet the train.

During the short journey I began to relax and was easily able to talk about the whole series of events. I knew by now that the nightmare was over. Neither Len nor Carl could ever do me any harm again, but the memory of the attempts they'd made would stay with me for a long, long time.

"We should have suspected him," Judy said. "He must have shot at Gracie and creased her. He couldn't very well shoot you and have your death judged to be accidental. But he creased Gracie because he knew she'd be temporarily paralyzed by the wound and go down so hard you'd be thrown and break your neck. He couldn't kill Gracie. He could kill people, but not a horse. I'm sorry for him."

"Perhaps I will be some day," I said. "Right now I remember too well how he searched for me in the forest that day. He would have killed me if he'd found me. He fooled me too. When I first arrived, I thought he was the one man I could trust because he showed no resentment that Alex had left the farm to me."

"Perhaps he thought you'd be easy to handle. Right up to the time you and Jess uncovered Carl's horse and you insisted the horse would not be run. That's when he must have really gone crazy."

"He tried to kill me before that," I reminded her. "Or perhaps he was only trying to frighten me so I'd leave the farm and never return. My impression is that he would have liked to control, if not own, the place so there'd be interference from no one."

"We'll never really know," Judy said. "What about the race? Have you formed any opinion?"

"None. I know too little about horse races. From what I have been able to understand, Majesty will likely be the winner. Carl may win a great deal of money...."

"No," Judy interrupted me. "Even Gordon finally realized what a fraud the whole scheme was. He and Jess tried to arrange it so Carl wouldn't be able to run the horse, but that would have taken a commission meeting and there wasn't time. However, they did manage to see to it that word of this wonder horse got around and the betting changed. Carl won't win a fraction of what he hoped to."

"I'm happy about that," I admitted. "I only hope they don't give him a chance to get away. He's probably a more dangerous man than Len, because I don't believe he has any inhibitions about killing. Though Len didn't seem to have any either."

"After the race, if Carl wins, they will likely disqualify him after they learn all the facts of what he was trying to pull. That would leave your horse, or Jess's, as the winner. Gordon couldn't see much competition from anyone else."

"We can iron all that out later," I said. "When things quiet down and we can think straight."

We arrived in time to use the hotel room Judy had already checked into. We were able to find a precious few hours to sleep and we were both somewhat groggy when we were awakened in the morning by Gordon. Judy led him away from the room while I dressed and she informed him of Len's death and the circumstances surrounding it.

While she and Gordon were gone, a tap on the door brought Veronica in to see me. She hugged me tightly and she wept for Len, but her happiness at finding me alive seemed far greater than her sorrow.

"I was so afraid of him," she said. "He was like a madman after he locked you in the cedar closet. He told me he'd send someone back before we boarded the train. But he never did and he threatened to kill me if I said a word of it to anyone. I'm not a brave person, Amy. In fact, I've no courage at all. That left me with the death of my husband and the loss of my three sons. But I meant you no harm. I swear it."

"I know you didn't," I comforted her. "I've known that all along."

"I wasn't sure if my sons were murdered, or

whether they died by accident. If it was murder, I thought Gordon must be responsible. He did covet the farm so. And I feared him. If he had killed my sons, he would easily kill me without the slightest compunction."

"It's over with me. I'm glad Gordon was not involved. It was bad enough that Len let his greed, or his love of horses, shade his thinking."

"If I'd suspected Len it wouldn't have been so bad, but I gave no thought to his guilt. I couldn't bear to accuse Gordon, so I began drinking. That was well before you met Alex. While he was still on the farm, in fact. Sometimes I think he left because of me. I drank and drank. When I was frightened, I drank. When I grew worried, I drank, and finally I just drank for no reason at all. I'm dreadfully ashamed of myself and have made up my mind I shall not drink again."

"Then you've won a serious battle of your own," I said.

"I hope so. Now that I think back and know the truth I thought Gordon was short and sometimes cruel with me because he thought I knew his secret. Now I think it was more a repugnance that my drinking caused. I made my peace with him last night. We'll be fine now."

"At least that much good came from this," I said. "I'm sure you'll be fine from now on."

She left me to get dressed. I had breakfast sent to my room and Judy soon joined me at the table.

"Gordon knows the whole story," she said. "He intends to apologize to you for the way he treated you. He means it. And he promised to devote more time to making Veronica happy. I liked that. Veronica is a fine person."

"She was here," I admitted. "We had a good talk. The only thing left now is the race and the hope that Carl will neither win nor get away from the race. He could be dangerous if he did."

"Indeed, for he is a spiteful little man. He hates me with the same devotion he's shown toward hating you. If he does manage to elude the police, I suggest we lock ourselves in our room and stay there until he is captured."

"We'll have to do something," I agreed. "How do I look, Judy?"

"Like you've attended the Cumberland for many years. You're right in style. My dress is last year's. I only hope no one notices."

"Not likely they will, for it's a beautiful dress, Judy. I'm ready now, if you are."

12

Judy, Veronica, Gordon, and I entered the brand-new, huge, twin-towered clubhouse. Gordon was well-known and we were greeted on every hand by people wishing to know the probability of Valiant again winning the Cumberland Stakes. We were in time to enjoy a light lunch, and amid all this confusion, gaiety, fashion, perfume, and flowers, what had happened yesterday seemed remote and all but forgotten.

The whole area was packed with landaus, phaetons, buggies, carriages, and even a few motorcars. The crowds were intense and devoted to enjoying themselves above all else.

We learned that betting was quite heavy on Valiant and only slightly less so on Jess's entry. The odds on Carl's horse seemed to come down every few minutes. But, actually, as Gordon put it, the betting was different this race. The money seemed to be far more well distributed than he'd anticipated.

"It's like nobody quite knows what to do," he explained. "They don't even seem particularly interested in that life-size statue of Valiant back of the clubhouse. I was certain that would ensure a great deal of betting our way."

As we mingled with the crowds heading for seats, I heard someone shout and Jess came elbowing his way through them. Without hesitation and little thought I found myself willingly in his arms, and when he kissed me, I returned it with more passion than I intended.

"I was afraid you might be in trouble," he explained. "Word reached me that Len is dead and I know the plainclothes police are watching Carl. I'm not sure he's aware of it, they seem careful in not letting him out of their sight."

"Oh, Jess," I said, "so much has happened. Some of it evil, some of it so good. Can we go somewhere and talk?"

"I can't," he said. "I have to be at the stable. The call for riders up will come soon now. There'll be a short parade as the horses are led to the track. I have to be there. I'm terribly sorry. May I see you after the races?"

"Jess, wait until it's all over and we're home again. Then please come and call on me. I'll look forward to it."

"No matter whose horse wins?" he asked with a grin.

"Horses are no part of this," I said. "I'm thinking only of you."

He leaned forward and kissed me again. "You've never been out of my mind, Amy. You never will be."

He hurried away and I looked for Judy, Gordon, and Veronica. We took our places in the stands. The parade to the track began and I had to admit that Valiant was a likely-looking horse. The animal seemed as enthralled by the excitement as we, and its thoroughbred heritage showed in his nervousness.

"Jess has a good-looking animal," Gordon said, "but I don't think he'll win. Here comes Carl, riding his own horse. Or the horse he thinks is his own. I'll swear it was sired, foaled, and trained on Greenlawn, with Len directing the whole thing and keeping the animal secret from all of us until a few weeks ago."

"I'm sorry Len isn't here," Veronica said. "No matter what he did, no matter what kind of a man he was, this race would have been the culmination of his career. He never looked forward to anything with more pleasure."

"And that," Gordon said grimly, "is part of his punishment."

Gordon handed me field glasses, and when the race began, I followed the horses as best I could. For an amateur I think I did rather well. But what hopes I had may not have been the high ones of the rest of my party, but they were dashed as completely. During the race Carl was forced against the rail and held there by other jockeys, particularly those who realized they had no chance.

"Carl's getting what he deserves," Gordon said. "They've got him trapped against the rail. Majesty can't get up speed. If he tried to ride out from that bunched-up mass of horses, he'd get killed. For once his reputation got the best of him. He can't win. And I'm not sorry."

"Valiant is not doing too well," Judy exclaimed in some dismay. "Jess's hasn't much of a chance either. There's a horse running a length and a half ahead and they can't catch up."

"Sir Huron," Gordon groaned aloud. "I've been afraid of that entry right from the first. That's a mighty fine piece of horseflesh, let me tell you."

"Sir Huron is going to win." Judy sighed. "He has won."

I lowered my glasses. "I'm sorry," I said. "Perhaps if Len had been here it would have been different."

"Not a chance," Gordon told me. "Our horse, Jess's horse, every horse in this race never had a chance. Sir Huron clocked in just over two minutes. I think that's close to a track record."

"Then we've lost everything?" I asked, in my ignorance.

"The devil we have," Gordon said. "We lost what we bet, but let me tell you our horse did very well, and remember, he won last year. We can stand this loss because that horse at stud will be in demand. We'll make up what we lost on the race and a lot more. Besides, we've got the horse Carl rode, and next year . . . we'll see."

"And Jess's horse?" I asked.

"Like ours. Didn't have to win, just to show what he had."

"You like Jess, don't you?" Veronica asked. She seemed wholly at ease now, as if a great weight had been lifted from her mind.

"Yes," I admitted. "Yes, I like him."

"He's a fine young man. Alex liked him too. My son would be very happy if—well, it's none of my business. I wish someone would take me out of this crowd."

Two days later everything came to an end. Len had been buried, in the family graveyard on the premises. Buried with the three brothers whose deaths he had either been responsible for directly, or had ordered them.

In death we forgave him everything. Carl had been arrested at the track and he'd confessed to the whole sorry episode in the hope his life might be spared by a jury. He was to be tried within the month and no one held out much hope for him.

He also admitted that Majesty belonged to Greenlawn, secretly foaled there, raised and trained without anyone except Len being the wiser. Had he won the race, he would have been disqualified.

We licked our wounds—the losses in betting at the track—and prepared to make Greenlawn a great success. By now I was as intrigued with the raising and training of horses as everyone else. There was only one provision that I secretly nurtured, for it was not mine to fulfill.

Only Jess could do that. He rode over as soon as he cleared up his responsibilities at the track and brought his horse home safely.

Judy saw him coming. I went out to meet him. No one accompanied me. Jess and I walked down to the stable, and Gracie was saddled. We rode out over familiar trails and we talked little. Until we reached a picnic spot, often used in the summer. There were tables, benches, and what we sought most, a privacy we wished to share together.

"I'm in love with you," he said. "I have no right to betray the respect you must feel for Alex, but it is my hope that one day . . ."

"Alex is dead," I said. "He would not wish me to act as if I were also dead. He would have wished me to be alive and happy—and in love. For I am, darling Jess. I love you as I once loved Alex."

He took me in his arms and for a long time we said nothing. Until I broke away from him gently.

"Would you care for proof that I'm in love with you, Jess?"

"Why do I need proof? I know you are. It's the happiest day of my life. I want to marry you. Soon. Would you marry me . . . very soon?"

I said, "Tomorrow I shall pay a visit to my lawyer. I made a will some time ago when my life was threatened. I made you my sole heir. I intend to change that will now."

"I think you should," he said.

"It's for a different reason, darling, than you think.

I am deeding the entire farm over to Gordon, Judy, and Veronica."

"What a generous gesture," he said. "But you must have a reason."

"I'm going to be in direct competition with Greenlawn," I said. "I'm going to help you make your farm the best in the state. Help you win, perhaps not the next Cumberland, but one very soon. And all the other races you choose to enter."

"We can do it together," he said confidently. "No question."

"Then let's change the subject from horses and racing to something even more important. The nightmare is over. Now we can dream—about us. Don't let go of me for a long time, darling. I feel safe now, in your arms."

SIGNET Gothics by Caroline Farr

- [ ] **SECRET AT RAVENSWOOD** (#E9181—$1.75)*
- [ ] **ROOM OF SECRETS** (#E8965—$1.75)*
- [ ] **DARK CITADEL** (#Y7552—$1.25)
- [ ] **ISLAND OF EVIL** (#W8476—$1.50)*
- [ ] **HEIRESS OF FEAR** (#W8300—$1.50)*
- [ ] **SINISTER HOUSE** (#W7892—$1.50)
- [ ] **CASTLE ON THE RHINE** (#W8615—$1.50)*
- [ ] **SIGNET DOUBLE GOTHIC—WITCHES' HAMMER and GRANITE FOLLY** (#J8360—$1.95)*
- [ ] **SIGNET DOUBLE GOTHIC—HOUSE OF DARK ILLUSION and THE SECRET OF THE CHATEAU** (#E7662—$1.75)
- [ ] **CASTLE ON THE LOCH** (#E8830—$1.75)*
- [ ] **CASTLE OF TERROR** (#E8900—$1.75)*

*Price slightly higher in Canada

Buy them at your local bookstore or use this convenient coupon for ordering.

THE NEW AMERICAN LIBRARY, INC.,
P.O. Box 999, Bergenfield, New Jersey 07621

Please send me the SIGNET BOOKS I have checked above. I am enclosing
$_____ (please add 50¢ to this order to cover postage and handling).
Send check or money order—no cash or C.O.D.'s. Prices and numbers are subject to change without notice.

Name _____

Address _____

City_____ State_____ Zip Code_____

Allow 4-6 weeks for delivery.
This offer is subject to withdrawal without notice.